Dedication

This book is dedicated to my son Nehemiah. You are the best thing that has ever happened to me. When I look into your eyes my problems become irrelevant. You make this process all the more special.

Love, Daddy

ENTREPRENEUR

A NOVEL BY M.Q.W.

Entrepreneur©

Entrepreneur

This is a work of fiction. The events and characters described here are imaginary and are not intended to refer to specific places or living persons.

Published by: 5ive Star Publications
Written by: M.Q.W.
Edited by: Shon Bacon for CLG Entertainment/www.clg-entertainment.com
Cover Design by: Anita Gillespie, aagille@hotmail.com
Typesetting and Layout by: Shawna Grundy, sag@shawnagrundy.com

For More Information Contact:
5ive Star Publications
P.O. Box 9176
Wilmington, DE 19809
E-Mail: mqw@5ivestarpublications.com
Website: www.5ivestarpublications.com

For Manuscript Submissions:
mqw@5ivestarpublications.com

Library of Congress Control Number: 2008912242
ISBN-10: # 0-9822638-0-5
ISBN-13: # 978-0-9822638-0-8
Printed in the United States of America
Revised Edition

ENTREPRENEUR

Acknowledgements

I first wanted to think my mother Martha for being my reason to keep going. I know she is watching over me everyday. Every time things become too hard I know I can see her face in the sky. I miss you Mommy and this is my gift to you.

The responses I got when I told people I was writing a book were funny. The responses I got when I told people I started a publishing company were even funnier. I used all that negative energy to fuel my story. Trust me there was a lot of it. I also learned that if you believe in yourself people will follow suit. My oldest brother Keith is the person that got me interested in pursuing my dreams. I seen him being an entrepreneur and I wanted to be just like him. The vision I saw was getting to the top and pulling people up. That's why I started 5ive Star Publications to do just that. I have a unique set of family and friends who all played a part in this.

My sister and three brothers have all inspired me. Jamal, I love you for being outspoken and true to being you no matter what. What up BG, I know our relationship hasn't always been great. The fact of the matter is you're my brother at the end of the day. I'm proud of you if nobody else tells you. Forget the past and let's embrace the future.

Marquita, I wanted to tell you that I'm always here for you. You know I know what you've been through in your life. I hope you look at this book as a way to follow your dreams. Sturg, I told you what I was trying to do. I told you I had this dream and you believed me. Thanks for sticking to your opinion always. I know that if I need the truth you will give it to me.

My parents Shirvell and Keith played a huge role in molding me into the man I am today. I took their success and failures and used it as a blueprint for what I do. I know that everyday isn't perfect, but I wouldn't trade either one for anything. They know the chances and risks I took in my life. Whenever I needed guidance they offered it. I hope I made ya'll both proud. Aunt Belinda if your reading this, I wanted you to know that I love you. You were like another mother during my childhood. You can think of me as one of your children. You made summertime an event. To be honest I miss going on those Wildwood trips.

Aunt Patty you left us too soon. I just wish we could go to the boardwalk and have fun again. You would have been proud of your nephew. This book is dedicated to you and all the other people who have left us too soon over the years. Sharmina, You were there when I was sitting at my laptop at 3 a.m. writing this book. Many people aren't blessed with a support system. I am blessed that you are apart of mines. You were there during my darkest hours. You know how many times I got frustrated with lack of movement, and you talked me into calming down. I wanted you to know that you are irreplaceable. I love you with all my heart. It's time to take it to the top.

I wanted to send a special shout out to Xanyelle from Horizon Books in Philly. I did my first book signing there and she made me feel comfortable and welcomed. Thank you. Also I wanted to thank Davida Baldwin of Oddball Design for creating my 5ive Star logo. Anita, you came just in time. I was looking hard for a graphic designer and we got linked up. You are a talented woman and I want to thank you for bringing my vision to life.

Shon, I wanted to thank you for sticking with me throughout the whole process. I learned so much about editing that I didn't know before. The most important thing is patience. When I bought Entrepreneur to you it was incomplete. Now I know that it is something special. Lastly I want to thank every reader that purchased the first version of Entrepreneur. Now I present you with the revised version. The decision to re-release Entrepreneur was an easy one. There were a lot of things that I was not feeling on my first go round. I acquired some talented people who helped me shape Entrepreneur into what I knew it should be. I hope you enjoy reading it as much as I did writing it.

And as always post your comments via Amazon.com or to me personally at mqw@5ivestarpublications.com.

Peace and God Bless.

-M.Q.W.

THE PRELUDE
SWIFT

I made it to graduation, and damn was I glad to go. I had spent six years of my teenage life at this private school. My stepmother, Camille, was in the army, so that enabled me to go away to school. Pops didn't care either way, as long as I got a decent education. I didn't want to go, but what choice did I have? I remember like it was yesterday, packing my bags for the three-hour trip to the middle of nowhere.

"Swift, get down here before we're late," my mom yelled up the stairs.

"I'm coming!" I lied, knowing damn well I wasn't ready.

"If you're not down here in five minutes, we're leaving you here," my mother threatened.

That would be a great idea, I thought.

I hustled down the stairs of our apartment building. When I got outside, I took one last look at the apartment building and sighed. My mother popped the trunk, and I threw my suitcase in. As I got comfortable in the car, I was mad all over again. When I looked at my brother, he had a stupid grin on his face.

I mustered up some confidence and asked my mother, "How come Malik not coming?"

"His dad doesn't want him to go," my mother said in that

parent tone I'd grown accustomed to hearing.

"That's an excuse?" I said, sounding disrespectful. As soon as I said it, I wish I could have taken my statement back. I swore my mother's hand moved in slow motion as she smacked the feeling out of my face. My mother's facial expression changed as my statement had hit a nerve. Malik's father, Raheem, was a worthless excuse for a father. All he did was send cards with no money and show up once in a blue moon. He was full of broken promises.

He still tried to make decisions for his son. After all, he was Malik's biological father. Pops locked the house up, then opened the car door and got in. He sensed something happened right away.

"Camille, what's going on?" Pops asked with concern in his voice.

"Nothing, honey," my mom said, not even giving him eye contact.

"Aight," he said skeptically. Then, he saw my brown face red and almost snapped. He knew what the deal was. Every time Raheem's name got brought up, all hell broke loose. He decided to drop the matter for the moment, but I knew he fully intended to sit down with Camille and discuss it by the way he looked over at her.

My mother put the key in the ignition, started the car, and put her Slick Rick CD in the disc player. The rest of the trip, I looked out the window. I was trying to be positive about my situation. I was thinking about the girls and what they would look like. I used to love when my mom had her book club meetings. I would sneak a peek at my mother's best friend, Ms. Peaches. She had to have the biggest breasts ever without being sloppy. I had to admit that the basketball thing did interest me, too. I'd been playing basketball since I could pick one up.

While we were driving, all I saw were highways and trees.

I was growing impatient with each passing minute. I kept shifting positions in the backseat of my mother's car. She kept shooting me that "Sit still" look. That was until I noticed we were closing in on my school. It was even better than seeing the glossy pamphlet pictures. Some places always tried to false advertise. Just like fast-food restaurants, they didn't look anything like the picture on display.

This place was different though. As we entered the school premises, I noticed the football team on the practice field. Their red and white uniforms appeared to be brand new, even from a distance. The field damn near resembled the football stadiums I saw on television most Sunday afternoons. There were numerous seats, all highlighted by the gigantic nightlights in back of the commentary booth. We pulled up to the tall, brown, brick building that housed the superintendent's office. I was a little shook. *What if I wasn't private school material?* I mean, I was an above average student, but who knew?

When my family and I entered the building, I noticed large-framed pictures on the walls of former students and staff members. The carpet was dark gray and spotless. Every office in the building had silver nameplates with employees' names etched into them. Even the water fountains seemed special for some reason. My mother mouthed, "Come on," as I wandered the lobby enjoying the scenery.

When we finally entered Superintendent Allen Thompson's office, I was relieved. He seemed like a cool person. He was even taller than Pops. He was an older gentleman with a gut problem far as I could see. Mr. Thompson wore glasses and was balding a little on top. His office bookshelves were lined with numerous books that interested me. I spotted *Native Son,* only because I had read it three times at the Free Library on 52nd and Market.

We all sat there as we introduced ourselves to the super-intendent. He shook my hand last, and proceeded to ask me questions. I told him my favorite hobbies were basketball and computers. He told me that there were plenty of basketball courts and computers to go around. Maybe it wasn't going to be bad after all. Then, Mr. Thompson asked, "Stephen, what do you think this school can offer you?" He said that as he sat on the edge of his desk with his hands in his lap. I was a little dumbfounded and caught off guard. I couldn't think of a good lie, so I just told him what I really felt.

"The opportunity to become an entrepreneur," I stated, smiling from ear to ear. My mother, Malik, and Mr. Thompson shared a laugh. I didn't see a thing funny. I was dead serious. I learned real young I wanted my own things. I didn't like my parents bossing me around. I wanted to be independent someday. I looked over at Pops and he nodded. I knew I had his silent approval. That trumped all the negativity in the room. Little did they know, their remarks gave me motivation.

After our session with Superintendent Thompson, we went to take a look at the housing units. Every patch of grass that I saw was cut perfectly. Not one piece of trash was on the ground. We backed out of the spot and drove across the beautiful campus. We passed the dining hall, hospital, and Superintendent's quarters. We pulled up to the back of the housing units and there were several other cars parked. Pops grabbed my suitcase and we entered my housing unit through the kitchen. When we got into the living room pass the dining room, there were balloons and a huge "Welcome New Students" banner.

A tall, skinny woman came around the corner and seemed to light up the room.

"Hello. My name is Lanay Bynum and I will be your child's houseparent," she said, extending her hand to Camille. She shook it back returning the smile.

Ms. Bynum took us on a mini tour, showing us the bathroom, basement, foyer, and living room. The living room had a 36-inch TV, three white couches, and a fake fireplace. We went upstairs and there were four rooms in all. My room was right next to the fire exit. Pops helped me unpack all my things. I lined my dresser with pictures of my family and put my fresh pairs of sneakers in the bottom of the small closet. I sat on the twin bed and noticed it was hard as hell right away.

My mother was on her cell phone and to me, it didn't even seem like she was there with us. I guess Pops caught my expression and patted the bed, signaling me to sit down. When Pops gave me his award-winning smile, my mood softened a bit.

"Swift, I know you don't want to be out here."

"Why you say that?"

He let out one of those laughs I knew too well.

"I mean, if I had a choice."

"This is something that is a lot better for you than you think. I know you think that it's a form of punishment, but trust and believe that we had several arguments over the final decision."

"You didn't want me to go, either?"

"To be honest, I thought that it was too far away. I wanted to see something that justified you going here. When I did my research, I found out a lot of positive things about the school."

"I guess I could give it a chance."

"That's all we ask. Aight, man, you all set up now. We gotta get back on the road before it gets too late." Pops lifted his sleeve to read his Movado watch.

I gave Malik a handshake and gave Pops a long hug.

"I love you, Pop."

"I love you, baby boy."

Camille gave me a hug, and it seemed genuine, which made me happy for the moment. I looked out the window until they all appeared out back. I watched them get into the car and watched until I couldn't see the brake lights anymore. I couldn't wait until Block came the next day. I knew me and him would get it crackin'.

As I was reminiscing, there was a knock at my room door.

"Yo, Swift, we got less than fifteen minutes to get to the stage," Kenny said, out of breath from running up three flights of stairs.

I grabbed my cap and gown and headed out. The graduation ceremony was just like I thought it was going to be. My whole immediate family was there, along with a couple of my aunts and uncles. My cousin, Mav, was there in the front row yapping away on his cell phone. Every time I looked off the stage, he was blowing kisses at the girls on stage. It was hard to contain my laughter.

Cars filled the area surrounding the stage. The banner on the top of the pillars behind us read, "Good Luck Class of 2002" in huge, red letters. The rows of seats were filled to capacity. When it was my turn to get my diploma, my family roared like I had won the state championship.

I just wished my biological mother, Rita, was there to see it. That brought a few tears to my eyes. She died during the pregnancy. Her and Pops were high school sweethearts. Me and my older brother, Keon, were the result of their marriage. It took a while for Pops to recover and eventually remarry. My youngest brother, Jahiem, came bursting into the world a short while after Pops and Camille's honeymoon.

That was the one thing that never stopped bothering me. On more than one occasion, I heard that I have to get over it speech. I carried it around with me wherever I went. I guess that was where my attitude problem came from. Sometimes, I was mad at the world. When I got older, I realized the world didn't do anything to me.

After the ceremony was over, I stood off to the side talking with my classmates. Soon as I was done and about to locate my family, I spotted Cianni. I gave her a hug and told her to keep in touch.

I let her perfume invade my nostrils. Her soft breasts rubbing against me reminded me of old times. It felt like she was still my girlfriend. The thing that got me was she understood what it was like coping with a tragedy.

Cianni and I both lost one of our parents. She lost her father when she was seven years old. She told me one day she came home and found him staring at her with gray, lifeless eyes. He was sitting in their recliner with a needle sticking out of his arm.

We had a special bond. It was far from just a sexual thing between us. When our parents' birthdays came, we did the same thing every year. We would let balloons loose in the sky and pray together.

Everything was good until I started showing out. I took the relationship for granted. After a while, I figured whatever I did she would be by my side. I knew she was getting tired of my inconsistent behavior. A couple times over our summer vacations, I stood her up on dates. I was busy trying my hand at different females.

When we got back to school, I ignored her sometimes for no reason. All I remember was her girlfriend giving me a note at lunch. I was thinking, *Why can't Cianni give it to me?* When I read it, I quickly found out why. She told me she loved me, but couldn't deal with me any longer. She wished me well, and told me to not speak to her again.

The majority of our senior year, we avoided each other at all cost. By the time graduation was approaching, we had resolved our differences. We agreed to keep in touch wherever we were.

Time sure does fly by.

Cianni had a baby girl now. She had her degree and was going to become a chiropractor. I saw her baby's father once back in high school. I didn't think homie was all that, either. Seeing her with a baby actually was bittersweet. I almost had one with her. When she went to have the abortion, I was trying to comfort her as best as I could.

I knew our parents would flip if they ever found out. We were so young and dumb. I knew that neither one of us could support a baby mentally or financially. So, we came to a mutual agreement to have the abortion. That was something that I kept from everybody, even Block.

This place held a lot of memories for me.

I had my first fistfight, my first sexual experience, and my first entrepreneurial dream started there. It was more than just a school to me. When the idea of bringing me here first came up, I thought it was a punishment. I soon realized it was actually beneficial in the long run.

I packed all my things in cardboard boxes and said my goodbyes. A lot of these people I would never see again. Some of them, I never wanted to see again anyway. I saw all the so-called popular dudes in high school and laughed to myself. Every memory that I had of school went through my mind like a slide show. I took in the buildings and the remaining people for one last time.

Superintendent Thompson was coming out of the building when I was about to get in the car. I debated whether or not to say something to him. On one hand, he was supportive when he wanted to be. I would always remember his sarcasm my first day there. I chose the mature route and approached him when he came toward me.

"Mr. Jackson, I just wanted to say congratulations on your graduation," Mr. Thompson said, extending his hand. I returned the gesture.

"Thank you, sir."

"You earned it. I remember like it was yesterday when you were in my office all the time."

"Things have changed since then," I said, getting a little defensive. Good thing my mother started the car, signaling me to come on.

"Well, thank you again, sir, and have a great night."

I opened the door and got comfortable in the backseat. My mother navigated back through the campus, passing by the scattered students that still remained. The sky was switching from blue to red to yellow. The clouds started to fade from the sky. The sight of that always relaxed me. I was in my own little zone as we drove through the farm land on either side of the road. We shared the road a couple times with other cars, sparingly, until we hit the highway. When we actually got on the highway, the cars were bumper to bumper.

Being fresh off graduation, I wanted to have some sort of fun. I was struggling to keep my eyes open and before I knew it, I was leaning against the window. I woke up to Malik tapping me.

"C'mon, Swift, we here."

"Where?"

"Bowling."

We were at Laurel Lanes in New Jersey. I rubbed my eyes and yawned before I finally got out the car. Pops went to the trunk and got a big duffle bag which held the bowling equipment. I made my way over to the double doors behind Malik and Camille. When I got inside, my aunt Dana and my uncle Ryan were there with my grandmother, Tia. They all started clapping and hollering at the top of their lungs when I rounded the corner. I was overcome with emotion. It made the accomplishment a little more special.

When I finally made it over to the table, it was filled with plastic bags and cards. I read all four cards and happily took the money that was stuffed in each one. The bags contained a pair of black Timberlands and a black State Property bubble coat.

I hugged everybody and took a seat on the uncomfortable plastic seat. Pops came around the corner with an ice cream cake and set it on the table. Pops then reached into his pocket and handed me a set of Maxima keys. The look on my face said it all.

"She's parked outside."

I jumped up and ran outside to the parking lot like a complete psychopath. I looked around frantically in the dark until I came across a black Nissan Maxima. It looked off the lot new. I unlocked the door and inhaled the brand new leather aroma. It smelled like a new pair of sneakers. It had a CD player and an AC. I was straight. I didn't have a license, yet, but I was still glad Pops got it for me. I locked it back and went back into the bowling alley.

Camille handed me my bowling shoes and I proceeded to switch shoes. Now, of course, Jahiem, Keon, and Malik started talking trash. They turned the lights down and put on the neon lights along side of the lane. I tied my shoes, being as though I was the first one up. I went and scanned the racks for a suitable ball. Once I got it, I was ready to beat each and every last one of them. We battled for three straight games. We talked trash, threatened each other's mothers, and put money on the games. I won the first one by one, the second one by twenty, and the last one by sixty. Pops couldn't stop laughing at how serious we were.

When I sat down, I drank three straight cups of Sprite. After I quenched my thirst, we all played one big family game. I loved every minute of it. After the game was over, they sung *Happy Birthday,* with graduation substituted in for birthday. I know that the other people thought we were retarded.

M.Q.W.

After we all ate some cake and embraced each other, we got ready to go. We all turned in our shoes and headed for the car. I caught up to Pops to ask him about the driving situation.

"Pops, what if I get pulled over?"

"You gon' have to learn how to drive sometime, right? Now is the perfect time. That is, unless you scared."

He knew I didn't back down from a challenge. I had watched Camille drive millions of times. It couldn't be that hard, right?

I got in the car, started it up, and waited for Camille to pull off. I was right behind her because I didn't want to lose her. I had never driven in Philly, let alone New Jersey. When I saw that oncoming traffic, I was shook. I kept my composure, considering that I was breaking the law and driving like a maniac. I prayed every five minutes that the cops didn't pull me over that night.

Chapter 1
Swift

Nearly a month had passed since graduation, and my mother was already sweatin' me. Normally, she was a sweet-looking woman, with her 5-feet-6, one hundred and seventy five pound frame and fudge complexion. She had jet black, shoulder length hair with bright eyes and long eyelashes. However, at that particular time, she looked like the devil, horns and all. Of course, she was on my case about employment. I was submitting applications left and right.

"Swift, get in this kitchen and wash these damn dishes," my mom shouted loud enough for the entire city of Philly to hear.

"Get him to do it," I mumbled under my breath. I gave Malik the ice grill as I passed the couch en route to the kitchen. I got in the kitchen and was able to count how many dishes were in the sink. There were two bowls, a plate, and three pieces of silverware. I think she yelled at Malik through me.

Everyday when I came home from community college, Malik was on the couch, hand in his boxers, watching MTV. It amazed me how lazy my brother was. My parents practically spoon fed him and that only made things worse. I could only shake my head in disappointment.

It was like every time I did something that wasn't up

to her grand standards, it was a problem. I could clean the house and if I happened not to mop that particular day, she bought it up. She tried to make it seem like I didn't complete anything. I couldn't remember the last time that Malik cleaned something. I would venture to say maybe when we were in 8th grade.

When I first came home, I could admit that I didn't want to do anything remotely close to constructive. When I realized that I wasn't making any money playing NBA Live, I started looking for employment anywhere I could. She was never on Malik's case about getting a job. Go figure, right?

I would be looking for a job and come home and see Malik smoking with the knuckleheads from around the way. They were a group of the smartest young brothers I knew. They just went down the wrong path and got caught up in what they thought was cool. When I went off to school, I desperately wanted Malik to come with me. Maybe if he came to school and saw what they had to offer he would have a different perspective on life. I couldn't understand for the life of me why he wouldn't use his GOD given abilities.

I went to my room to finish a term paper. I was the greatest procrastinator on planet earth. I had to type ten more pages, and I had to be in class at 10 a.m. sharp. I started to type the fastest I could with one finger. After awhile, I incorporated a finger on my left hand.

I looked down at the bottom right corner of my laptop and the time read 11:57 p.m. The next thing I remember was waking up to a string of mismatched letters as a result of falling asleep on the keyboard. I spent fifteen minutes deleting the letters. I wasn't even done typing my paper, and I wasn't surprised.

I ripped a black sweat suit off the hanger, laid it on my bed, and hopped in the shower. I took the quickest shower time would permit, and jumped into my clothes and boots. I sprayed on some Fahrenheit cologne and tied on my black do-rag. I put my laptop in my bag and ran up the basement steps clear across the living room out the door.

I didn't stop running until I was at the corner of 46th and Baltimore Ave. I could see the 34 trolley coming, and I was glad because I could barely breathe. I caught my breath soon as the trolley pulled up. I found a seat in the back by the window. I took out my laptop and took a deep breath before I attempted for a second time to finish this paper.

The trolley ride gave me just enough time to finish it. Just being in school was an accomplishment for me because I really didn't think I would even get a chance to go to college. My high school guidance counselor, Ms. Patterson, was on top of me every five minutes. I wasn't the easiest student to deal with. I had a study hall near the end of the day with her. She made sure that I finished whatever homework I had before I could leave for my last period class. I didn't appreciate how much she cared until I actually graduated.

I could have the worst attitude and it didn't matter to Ms. Patterson. She always kept a smile on her face. I could never get her rattled even though I tried my hardest to. I had a lot of trust in her because she had a real open door policy. There were plenty of times I went to just have a conversation about something bothering me. Her advice was priceless. There was a time when I thought that I was going to get kicked out of school until Ms. Patterson convinced the school otherwise. I just knew that it was over for me. I sat on the bed in my dorm room and couldn't believe I had jeopardized my whole future over a fist fight.

The tears were coming in buckets. I felt a hand on my shoulder, but I didn't move until I heard that familiar voice.

"Everything will be ok, baby."

All I could do was except her embrace.

"I messed up this time, didn't I?"

"No, baby, you didn't."

"Huh?"

"You just made a mistake, that's all."

"But, that mistake is going to get me kicked out of school."

"I told them I would quit before I let them kick you out."

"You did what?" I said, breaking the embrace.

"You heard me right." Ms. Patterson smiled.

"Thank you." I hugged her one more time.

She was the one who was on me about filling out college applications. At first, I had a lot of negativity toward it. I knew I wasn't an honor student, so why would a college want me? I feared rejection, so my thinking was that if I didn't apply I couldn't get turned down. After I put it off for as long as I could, I finally sat down with Ms. Patterson.

We searched the internet and read information books on the college application process. With the SAT scores I got, I was limited. I didn't bomb or anything, but I had a glass ceiling. It felt good to at least try, though. I had wasted phone cards telling Camille about my aspirations. She kept kicking me some garbage about not wasting her money on me. That alone made me want to quit the whole process. When I let Ms. Patterson know, she deaded all the negative energy.

I held my hopes high until I got home in the summertime. A week after I got home, I had three responses in the mail. I was with Block when I came home and checked the mailbox. I gave the envelopes to Block and asked him to open them. The first two were rejection letters. I would be lying if I said I wasn't expecting it. I stood for the first two, but my energy was zapped after that. I mentally crossed my fingers, hoping someone took a chance on me.

"Well, you want to hear the good news or the bad news first?"

"Bad news," I said, preparing for the worst.

"First and foremost, them first two schools ain't too bright for not accepting you."

"What's the good news?" I said, finally looking up.

"This school a little brighter," he said, smiling.

My face lit up instantly. I got up and gave Block dap and a hug. I was so excited. I just knew that it was my time.

We all even went to visit the potential school. I'll never forget the day. I was hype. I woke extra early like they were going to actually leave me. We made the drive to Summerdale, PA to Central Pennsylvania College. I read the pamphlet like a little kid. I made sure that I didn't miss a bit of info. It was almost identical to my school's campus. We pulled into the parking lot in the front and made our way to the front desk.

We all took a seat and waited for our tour guide to come. A tall, white man with glasses, which he adjusted every five minutes, came and greeted us warmly. We went everywhere from the gym to the student apartments. The apartments were just the right size and featured stainless steel appliances, wall to wall carpeting, central air, and two bathrooms. I spoke to the students who were all draped in college colors. It made me want to enroll that second. I was feeling the whole experience. The campus was perfect and I could see myself graduating from there. When we got back home that night, I had no idea that my dreams weren't going to come true.

After a few heated arguments with my mother, I knew she had no intention of putting the money up for me. I was so pissed I couldn't put it into words. That's when I called Ms. Patterson and she put me down with the Community College of Philadelphia. She knew somebody in admissions and sent them my transcripts. I still had to put the work in, though. I passed both of the qualifying tests with flying colors. I felt proud to be on the verge of graduating again.

The trolley pulled up to 19th Street and stopped. I closed my laptop, picked up my book bag, and went up the steps. There were hoards of people walking back and forth, crowding the sidewalk. I made the two-block walk to catch the bus to Spring Garden Street. I dodged a few oncoming cars and got to the bus stop. After about ten minutes, the bus pulled right in front of me. Every single person there with me got on the bus, which was nearing capacity. I put my laptop in my book bag and took the only standing space available, which was right in the front next to the bus driver. I hated when the bus was that crowded. I could barely even swipe my transpass. Good thing the ride wasn't that long.

The bus abruptly pulled up to the corner when someone hit the yellow strip. I got off and made the walk to class. There were students everywhere. I had to navigate trough the crowd just to get something to eat. I bought me a bacon, egg, and cheese on a hoagie roll and a grape can soda. I sat on the bench and ate before my class started. I knew that Mr. French would blow his top if I was late again. I finished up my sandwich and went in early just to play it safe. If I didn't go in now I was done for.

I went through the double doors and got on the escalator. I looked over at the escalator going down at the girls who were smiling at me. I had a fresh shapeup just for that purpose. I couldn't get enough of them. I got off the escalator and went across the hall. There were a few students sitting and talking. It was just my luck Mr. French walked in soon as I did.

I sat my book bag down and went to the student lounge to print my term paper. I sat down and checked it one more time for accuracy and was satisfied with it. I plugged my laptop up to the printer and waited for it to finish printing. Once it did I stapled it twice. I worked hard on it and hoped that Mr. French recognized it, too. I walked back to his room, sat down, and let out a deep breath. I needed at least a B to walk across that stage. The anticipation was killing me.

Chapter 2
Block

Block woke up in the king-sized bed occupied by two beautiful, redbone women. Out of habit, he checked his clip.

"Sixteen shots," Block said to no one in particular.

After his gun inspection, he went into the hotel bathroom to brush his teeth. Block really admired the beautiful suite setting. They had Veuve Clicquot Yellow Label champagne on ice in the fridge. It had a full kitchen, two bathrooms, and a full bar. It was fit for a king, and Block was one. It wasn't bad for a kid in his early twenties.

Block was thrown from his thoughts when he saw something that caught his eye. The box of Cohiba cigars from the club were on the sink. He immediately remembered where he'd met the women. The 40/40 Club in New York.

He had called up Trill, Stack, and Swift and told them to meet him at his shorty's crib just off City Line Avenue. When Block saw his boys roll up, they all came in for a quick second. Block introduced them all to Chante and stepped off for a second. He left them downstairs and went to get his gun. He put the clip in and slid the top back. Then, he put the black handgun in his waistband and went back downstairs.

When they got outside, his crew's mouths hung wide

open. He pushed a button sequence that lifted the garage door to reveal a black Infiniti QX56 truck.

"This fool cops a car every week, don't he?" Swift said, tapping Trill.

"He damn sure do," Trill said.

"You know how I do," Block said, tapping the truck's hood.

"Here we go again," Trill and Swift shouted in unison.

There were so many people in Times Square you could barely see the ground. The lights from the numerous signs and billboard advertisements were extra bright that night.

After Block paid the attendants to park their vehicles, the quartet walked a few blocks to the W hotel and paid for their individual hotel rooms. The hotel clerk smiled and handed them each a white key card. They took the escalator and were back out on the street in no time. When they finally got close to 6th Avenue, women were everywhere. Groups of women were strutting in front of them, waving at the young men. They couldn't wait to get inside and enjoy themselves.

Soon as they got near the front door, it was wild. The line was long, and they could see people getting frustrated at the lack of movement. Block knew the bouncer, Elz, so they skipped the line and the pat down. The chiseled bouncer stepped aside, and the crew strolled in the spot. You couldn't even put your hands in your pocket. It was that tight in there. Block's crew split up, and he made a beeline to the bar area.

As Block was playing the bar, he saw some women, but nobody really caught his eye at first. He proceeded to order a box of Cohiba cigars and an $800 bottle of Ace of Spades Rose. The bartender popped the cork for Block and he tipped her $200. She tried to hide the excitement, but still gave him a "you can have it right now" look.

As Block drank from the bottle, he spotted the two women

dancing with each other. They were dancing real sensual, grinding and grabbing each other. He definitely took notice. He needed both of those women in his bed. When one of them came to the bar giggling, he took a shot. He was facing her side when he spoke.

"What you drinking, miss?"

Ending the small talk with the chubby bartender, she spun around. Once Block flashed his eggshell white smile, he could have sworn she had an instant orgasm right there on the barstool. She couldn't help but stare at his dark skin and perfectly lined shapeup that led to his full beard. He smelled great and his shoes were spotless. She mentally crossed things off her must have list.

"Whatever you're buying," she said bluntly. He ordered her two Jolly Ranchers.

"Where ya dance partner go?" he said, flashing his smile again.

"Oh, my cousin, Keisha, she went to the bathroom," she said, flashing a perfect white smile of her own. "Where you from, sexy?"

"Illadel, shawty," Block said proudly, pointing to the tattoo of Philly's skyline on his muscular right shoulder. "Where you from?"

"Jersey City."

"More importantly, what's ya name, ma?"

"Cashrondra, and yours?"

"Block." He decided not to beat around the bush. "How 'bout you and your cousin come to my hotel suite?"

"I don't know. I'll think about it, cutie," she purred.

"Aight, well if y'all do, that's cool, but if not, it's all love."

With that, he left his room key at the bar and then bounced in search of his boys. He walked through the crowded club scanning for them. When he caught up to them, they were playing the dance floor hard.

"Yo, I'm out."

"You good?" Trill asked while looking over the shoulder of a female.

"Yeah, I'm straight. It's just I'm 'bout to ménage wit' a couple freaks. Make sure them two drunk fools get home safe," Block said, pointing to Swift and Stack. They both were grinding on females with drinks in their hands.

"I got you," Trill said.

"One-Hun-it."

"Girl, who was that?" Keisha asked Cashrondra as she returned from the bathroom adjusting her hair and skirt.

"Our next victim, that's who," Cashrondra shouted. They laughed, then high-fived each other. Block looked back and saw her snatch the card off the bar. He smiled, adjusted his Louis Vuitton shades, and strolled outside.

Block made the short walk back toward the hotel. The night air was crisp and the champagne had Block on chill, but he was always on alert. He patted his waist just to confirm his gun was still there. The feel of the heavy steel made Block feel safe.

Heading to his hotel suite, Block strolled off the elevator like he owned the hotel. In a couple quick strides he was at his door. He entered his suite and went straight to the king sized bed, bypassing the window that offered a great view of the city. He kicked off his Louis Vuitton loafers and lounged back on the bed. Before he knew it, his eyes were closing. Then, he was lightly snoring.

The door's click made Block wake up instantly and reach for his gun. He laughed when he realized it was his company. He quickly slipped two Listerine strips on his tongue.

They both made their way to the doorway and gave Block seductive stares. Their plan was to hold nothing back. They slowly walked to the edge of the bed. Keisha was the boldest out of the two. She grabbed Block's face with both hands and stuck her tongue in his mouth as she kissed him slowly. He grabbed her waist, pulling her to him. He eventually located her softness, squeezing it.

Cashrondra, not to be left out, hurried Block out of his pants. She massaged his shaft until it rose to life. She looked at it like it would never stop extending. She moistened her lips and put soft kisses on the top of it.

Cashrondra and Keisha both got up and began to undress each other slowly. Cashrondra stood 5'7', coffee brown, and extra curvy. Her huge breasts made Block's mouth water. Keisha had a peanut butter complexion and was pole thin until you got down to her hips. How she could be skinny and thick at the same time; Block couldn't figure out.

Keisha pushed both of Cashrondra's 46DDD breasts together and swirled her tongue around her dark areolas before savoring her succulent cocoa nipples. When she bit them lightly, it sent Cashrondra into a frenzy. Block couldn't take it any more and swiftly joined in on the action. He laid Keisha on the bed and spread her legs wide. She grabbed her own ankles, seemingly pulling them apart even further. He positioned himself behind Cashrondra, rubbing his tip on her now bubbling vagina.

At the same time, Cashrondra began to make lunch of Keisha's moist triangle. She licked every spot imaginable between her thighs except her clit. She darted her long tongue in and out of Keisha until the sheets were damp with her essence. Satisfied that she had her on edge, she flicked her tongue across her clit as it grew twice its normal size.

Block watched the work that Cashrondra was putting in and slid inside her with little effort. A moan escaped Cashrondra's lips as she pulled her mouth off of Keisha. Soon as she felt Cashrondra's tongue move, she directed her right back to her sticky bull's eye. After a few more minutes of oral pleasure, she stopped Cashrondra.

Keisha positioned herself behind Block. As he was giving it to Cashrondra, she would periodically pull his shaft out and clean it off before putting it back inside Cashrondra.

They switched positions a few more times before the trio was too tired to continue. Cashrondra and Keisha fell asleep, holding each other. Block reached over on the nightstand and grabbed a Cohiba cigar and lit it up. He went over to the fridge and popped a bottle of champagne. He stepped out on the balcony, taking in the Big Apple. The sounds of blaring car horns never bothered him. He felt like a boss. He sat down, placing the bottle on the ground. He blew the smoke until it seemed to circle around him. He enjoyed the aroma of the expensive cigar. He took one more look at the girls and said to himself, "I love New York."

* * * * *

Bird sat in Maggiano's on 12th and Filbert picking through his lasagna. He had lost his appetite thinking over the money he was losing to Block's better product. The streets were definitely talking. Bear, his bodyguard, sat directly across from him. He kept his hands rested on the .38 snub in his lap. Thoro sat to his left and Speed sat to his right. They kept their eyes fixated on everything around Bird. They took his safety seriously. After pondering for the last half hour, Bird knew what he had to do. That put a smile back on his face.

He threw two hundred dollars on the table and gave a head nod. His crew got up and ushered him out the door like an A-list celebrity. Bear opened the almond-colored Bentley passenger door, then walked around and got into the driver side. Bird needed to see proof of the competition up close and personal.

Chapter 3
Swift

I had been ignoring my phone all day, but when I saw Keon's number flash I picked it up.

"Yo."

"Where you at?"

"At the crib, what's up?"

"I need to talk."

"Aight, give me fifteen minutes and I'll meet you at The Bridge."

I knew my brother wanted to talk business by the urgency in his voice. One of his patented get rich quick escapades was brewing. I pulled up to 40th and Walnut, and found a good parking spot around the corner from the movie theater.

Knowing Keon, he probably was running late as usual. So, I sat and thought of the last time my brother had a great money making idea. It was summertime when it happened. I remember because it was hot as hell in New York. Had to be at least ninety seven degrees out there. As we cruised the highway, I became cynical.

"So, we can get these Jordans for $35?"

"Yeah, what, you don't believe me?" Keon said, acting as if he was offended.

"I mean, if it sounds too good to be true, it always is."

"I've done business with this cat, he good peoples. Matter fact, I set everything up already. You'll see it's all gravy when we get there."

I looked at Jalen, the driver, and confirmed my suspicions. His hands gripped the steering wheel tightly, and his eyes peered out the window nervously. Not to mention, he kept asking Keon, "This way, right?"

Jalen and my brother were good friends. Jalen was a college basketball star and took numerous beatings at the hands of my brother. He definitely earned his stripes on the Philly playgrounds.

When we got to the building, we were bombarded by bootleggers. They were carrying everything from Air Force Ones to cologne bottles. After we sat there for a minute, a Jamaican cat knocked on the window. We all exited the vehicle and headed to the fourth floor. Keon, Jalen, and the Jamaican cat engaged in small talk while I was lost in my own thoughts.

The elevator doors opened with a loud creak, and might I say the building had seen better days. The carpet was stained heavily, and the paint was chipped in damn near every spot. The hallway smelled of mildew and garbage.

"Okay, brotha, my price be $45," the Jamaican said.

"Hold up, on the phone you said $35," Keon said, damn near screaming. At 6-feet-4, two hundred and forty pounds, he wasn't to be played with. The Jamaican cat must have gotten the point.

"How many pairs of shoes you want?"

"I need ten pairs on discount, feel me?"

With his accent in full swing, he said, "Three-fifty."

"Cool."

We all chipped in, and Keon handed him the money.

"Wait here five minutes."

"Aight, but hurry up. We trying to get back to Philly," Keon shouted as the door closed.

Just like that, the Jamaican disappeared behind the white apartment door. We all stood in the hallway and bussed it up for a few minutes. Breaking the silence, I asked, "What MJ's we copping?"

"The number three's," Keon said.

I had noticed we had been in the hallway longer than I expected.

"Where ya boy at?"

"I don't know. He usually faster than this."

I realized he had played us. My mouth got dry, my stomach started to hurt, and my palms were sweaty. I knocked on the white door, and what do you know, it magically opened. We all went into the apartment in search of the Jamaican. What we found were shoeboxes lined against both sides of the walls, none of which contained sneakers, or anything else for that matter. I kicked the boxes in frustration.

Then, we all noticed the window that led to the fire escape. We knew the money was gone.

I was thrust from my thoughts as my cell phone vibrated. I flipped it opened and answered, "You here?"

"Yeah," Keon said. "I'm in the back near the other entrance."

"I'll be there in a minute."

My brother was there for me through thick and thin. Even though I endured some of his antics, he always had my best interest in mind. I entered the building past the theaters and concession stands and immediately spotted my brother. We sat on the barstools, and Keon got the attention of the bartender and ordered our food and drinks. After a bit of silence, Keon started his persuasive speech.

"I know this cat selling industrial size vending machines for $200 a piece."

"Can we make money?" I asked straightforwardly. My brother sometimes stalled when you asked him questions.

This time was no different, so I waited for an answer.

"Yeah, I mean, it's slow cake at first," he stated nervously, forcing a laugh.

"How slow?" I said, raising an eyebrow.

"We make our money back in a month tops. Plus, we go half on every machine."

We kicked it for the better part of an hour, eating and drinking. I had no idea at that moment our conversation would play a major part in my life.

After meeting with Keon, I went to get my weekly shape-up. Aaron's was the barbershop to go to. It was rated number #1 in the city twenty years in a row. Aaron's had framed pictures of superstar clientele. I had been going there since they gave you a damn lollipop after your haircut.

Pops said I never cried, not even when I was real little. I saw grown men cringe when the barber applied the alcohol to their neck. Aaron's was white and black in design. The back of the shop held state of the art shampoo sinks. The chairs had push button adjusters instead of the old school levers. They paid attention to each individual person. You felt at home and comfortable.

As expected, it started on cue.

"They gon' trade Allen this summer, damn it!" Aaron stated.

We had those debates every summer. Every summer, the Sixers shopped A.I. and then acted like they weren't trying to trade the franchise away.

The season barely started and already Aaron was going haywire. He was a Sixers fan to the death. One time he shaped Iverson up, and he always pointed to the autographed picture to prove it. He told us the story like we forgot the last forty five times he told us. I had to admit, it was entertaining and funny.

Just as I was about to give my two cents, something caught everybody's attention.

A champagne-colored Jaguar pulled up in front of the barbershop.

"Goddamn!" came the collective shout from the shop before everyone stood.

"Who that?" Aaron said.

"Man, that's Block," I said, getting out my seat.

Block had a confident swagger about him. He commanded your respect when he entered your presence.

"I ain't expect you 'til later," I said.

"I just came from my mama house. Take a ride wit ya boy," Block said, waving his hand toward the door.

"I'm next in the chair, come scoop me in like twenty minutes."

"Cool, I'll hit you on the cell on my way back," Block replied.

"Aight, my dude," I said, followed with dap.

Aaron gave me my usual shapeup after I got my hair braided by Lisa. I would let that girl grease my scalp every day of the week. Her hands were magic, and I almost fell asleep while she was braiding.

Block picked me up around 4:30 and we went to South Street. When I got in the Jag, I was amazed at all the features. The sun blocking flaps had TVs, and the dashboard and steering wheel were wooden. The state of the art stereo system definitely was on point. Block put in Kindred The Family Soul's CD, and we rode to the sounds of their single *Far Away.*

Soon as we got there, it was, of course, bananas. Women were looking through the dark tint like we were celebrities.

We were in standstill traffic for like fifteen minutes before Block snapped. "See, fam, when I come down here it's always the same thing."

"How long we been coming down here though? Every time we come to South Street, you say the same thing. You want to take the bus?"

"I been driving since I was fourteen. I'm not trying to ride public transportation ever again."

We finally found a parking spot off Bainbridge Street. By that time, we were both starving. We walked a couple blocks and finally decided on Ishkabibbles. I loved it there. The only thing was the damn line hung around the corner. After what seemed like years of waiting, we got to the counter. My mouth was watering as I ordered our chicken cheese steaks and gremlins. We walked back to the car and started tearing into our food. In between bites, Block started explaining his plan to me.

"As you know, I got Philly on smash." He wiped his mouth and studied me for an answer.

"So I heard."

"Well, I wanted to know if you was down to get that paper," Block said between sips of juice.

"I don't know, man. It's something I would have to think on."

After high school, he always tried to put me down, but I declined every time. That time, however, I was going to give it some thought.

CHAPTER 4
BLOCK

The day that Block was recruited started like any other day. He woke up, loaded his .45, and showered. He put on a fresh, out the plastic wifebeater, and then strapped on a double breasted bulletproof vest. He searched his closet for something quick to put on. He chose a pair of black and white Diesel jeans and a black hoodie with gray thermal lining. He laced up his white and black patent leather Jordans and his cipher was complete. He opened his nightstand drawer and grabbed a stack of hundred-dollar bills. He counted it out 'til he had $1,000. He folded it and put a rubber band on it. He checked his gear in the mirror, and walked into the living room.

He hated the cramped space that he and his mother shared. He stayed out late sometime just to avoid coming back there. Just so his mother wouldn't worry, he called her and gave her his e.t.a. every night he went out. The one thing he always had was respect. He knew she worried about what he did in the streets, but he never brought any type of drugs past her door. He didn't bring any of his girls in the house, either. Come to think of it, he didn't even raise his voice or cuss in front of his mother.

He made sure he cleared all the dishes and cleaned the

countertops until they were spotless. After he was done, he vacuumed the carpet seemingly in one motion. He knew the hours his mother worked and didn't want her to do any unnecessary labor.

He took ground beef out of the freezer and sat it in the sink to thaw. He quickly made some cherry Kool Aid. He tasted it and was satisfied it was sweet enough. He grabbed the keys to his truck and bopped out the door and downstairs. The sun was out and caused him to shield his eyes. The truck seemed to have that showroom sparkle even though its surroundings were filthy.

Block hopped in and pulled around the corner, leaving tire marks. He made the usual ten block trip and parked near the corner store. He got out, observing the streets thoroughly before entering the little corner store. Block went to the back and grabbed a 50-cent hug and a bag of barbecue chips. The Arabic owner gave him a fist-pound as he paid and then walked outside. His oldheads were setting up shop and he acknowledged them with a head nod.

He walked over to the truck and discreetly pulled the gun off his waist. He put it on top of the truck tire and walked back to his post. He ate his chips and drank his juice, never taking his eyes off his surroundings.

A black on black Maybach came to the middle of the strip, causing Block to suspiciously squint his eyes. The passenger observed Block make his move to grab his pistol. That caused the passenger to smile. He instructed the driver to pull up near the parked truck. Soon as the car came to a halt, the window slid down slowly.

With the gun at his side, Block spoke, "Go up the block, oldhead."

The passenger's laughter seemed to ring loudly in the early morning atmosphere. That pissed Block off even more. Seeing a commotion about to start, one of the lieutenants ran over to diffuse the situation.

"Chill, Block, he cool," the lieutenant said, forcing a laugh.

Caliente waved Block into the vehicle. He still eyed him cautiously. He reluctantly put his gun on his waist and got into the backseat.

"I've been hearing a lot about how you conduct business out here. You slow to talk and quick to shoot. I dig that. You gotta understand that this game is built on much more."

Block was half listening while admiring the interior of the car. It was almost as big as his and his mother's living room. The leather was soft and it smelled fresh. There sat a laptop, fridge, and small plasma TV. It made Block's truck look like a ten speed bike.

Catching Block checking out the car, Caliente said, "This is nothing. Running with me, you can have ten of these easy."

Block heard him, but he didn't trust anybody as far as he could throw them. He then caught the jewelry on his hands. He was having trouble looking directly at it. The diamonds had superior clarity. The pinky ring he had on was the size of a Lego piece. He kept his facial expression emotionless. He didn't want homie to think he was some sucker ready to jump headfirst into just anything.

The truth was, he knew what lifestyle he wanted. He felt that way since the day he got caught with E pills in his gym locker. They made a scene by dragging him out during lunch time. Nearly every student was there to see the arrest. There had to be at least six cop cars. The police always overdid things. In the papers, they had it like he was some kind of kingpin. They found a sandwich bag with less than ten pills. They were a joke.

While they were taking him away, he caught Swift's facial expression. He was leaving his brother and that really hurt him the most. He didn't care for his degree. He had all the knowledge he needed. It wasn't like he couldn't apply himself, he just didn't want to. He was addicted to the paper and the lifestyle that came with it. It was too much to turn down.

Caliente waved his hand and the driver pulled off. The car rode smoothly, even when they encountered Philly's notorious potholes.

"You hungry?"

"Naw, I'm straight."

When Caliente heard Block's stomach growl, he laughed out loud.

"Make this right up there."

Block could see William Penn and knew they were nearing Center City. It was like the people in the city were on a continuous loop. Every time he went down that strip it seemed like the same people were in the same spots.

Caliente instructed the driver to pull them in front of Ruth Chris Steakhouse. He knew the youngster had never been there before. He was putting on one hell of a front, but Caliente knew better. He could see it in his eyes. He was different than the people he came in contact with on a daily basis. He could tell he hated asking people for things. He was a go-getter. That title couldn't be given to just anyone. He just had an overall good feeling about Block. His gut never lied and he wasn't about to go against it now.

The Maybach came to a halt in front of the upscale restaurant. Caliente's driver got out the car, opening the door for Caliente and Block. The driver closed the backdoor and pulled off in search of a parking spot.

The two men stepped toward the door and an attendant held it open for them. Caliente stepped through like royalty. Block followed right behind him.

"Table for two?" the hostess asked.

"Yes, ma'am."

She grabbed two menus and led them to the eating area. Block noticed that nobody was in the restaurant except them. The hostess led them to a seat in the far left corner. The table had a spotless white cloth and a little lamp illuminating the little area.

"Your waiter will be with you in one moment. Enjoy your meal," the blonde-haired waitress said, then walked away.

Not even a moment later their waiter showed up.

"Can I start you gentleman off with anything to drink?"

"Yes, I will have a glass of Pinot Grigio."

"And you, sir?"

Block wondered if Caliente knew he was under age.

"He'll have a glass of Merlot," Caliente replied.

"Very well, I will get those right away."

As soon as the waiter was out of earshot, Block spoke.

"You got that much power?"

"I run this city. Anything I want is within my grasp. Money talks and it's a universal language."

The waiter came back, put the two glasses down, and pulled out his notepad.

"Will you gentlemen be having appetizers?"

"Yeah, but we'll take our appetizers and entrées together. I'll have the crabtini, cowboy ribeye, baked potato, and fresh asparagus.

"And, I'll have the lobster bisque, the New York strip, mashed potato, and creamed spinach."

"Excellent choices," the waiter said as he grabbed the menus and was off again.

Block looked around at the elegant set-up. This was what he wanted to do. He wanted to eat expensive food and drink expensive wines. He loved to read up on different countries. He knew that when he got to where he was going it was a done deal.

Both men sipped on their wines and had small talk until

the waiter came back with steaming hot plates.

All you could hear were the forks and knives scraping against the plates. Their conversation was cut short soon as the aroma entered there nostrils.

After their meals were done, they lit up expensive cigars. Block blew circles of smoke like he had been doing it for years.

"All this can be yours," Caliente said with a wave of the arm.

"At what cost?"

"Minimal."

"Look, where I am is comfortable. I'm not trying to complicate things."

"I understand your perspective. Who would want to mess up familiarity? I could put you in a position to be a millionaire in six months. I can give you financial security. All I ask is your loyalty."

Block sat there soaking in Caliente's proposal. Yeah, he made money, but it wasn't what he thought he should be getting. He was hesitant to take the offer, but Caliente wasn't taking no for an answer.

Block simply raised his hand and shook Caliente's, sealing the deal.

"I understand you are in school still."

"Yeah, I'm home on summer break."

"For right now, you will work for me on your holiday breaks as well as the summer. A higher position will be waiting for you when you graduate."

Caliente left a hundred and fifty dollar tip and the men were off. The hostess gave them warm smiles and another attendant held the door for them. The Maybach slowed down and stopped right in front of them. The driver got out and hurried to the back door. He opened it, allowing Caliente and Block to get in.

M.Q.W.

During the drive, both men were lost in their own thoughts. The once blue sky was now turning a shade darker, giving way to nighttime. The expressway was relatively empty for that time of night. Block looked up and saw the green signs displaying New Jersey but kept quiet. The driver turned right in the parking lot of The Crown Plaza Hotel. He doubled parked in front of the hotel and killed the engine.

"Now, I have prepared a gift for you to show my generosity. If I'm with you, then you are family," Caliente said, handing Block a keycard. Block took the card and tucked it into his pocket.

The driver came to the backdoor and opened it so Block could exit. Block hopped out, not really knowing what to expect. He stood there and watched as the luxury car peeled out of the parking lot, leaving him there alone.

He went through the doors entering the lobby. He bypassed check in straight for the elevator. He hit ten and the circle lit up red. He watched as the car went from floor to floor. He didn't know why the hell he was nervous all of a sudden. The day couldn't get crazier, right? The door opened, and Block stepped out and looked at the signs. He went down the corridor until he was in front of the door. He looked at the number on the keycard just to make sure he was correct. He slid the card in and entered the room.

Everything was quiet, which was kind of weird. Something made Block go into the bedroom. Soon as he cracked the door he saw it. There were four completely nude women. Two were lying on the bed and the other two were on both sides of the King-sized bed. Two more came out of the bathroom.

"Open that door," one of the girls said real seductively.

He did as he was told, reaching in the closet for the black suitcase that was sitting on the carpet. He cracked it open and it was filled with car keys and neat stacks of hundred-dollar bills. He snapped it shut and admired the six women up close.

The room fell silent until the same woman spoke again.
"Your wish is our command."
"Is that so?"
"Yes, Mr. Block."
There was no reason to speak another word.

Chapter 5
Swift

It turned out that I got an 81 on my final exam. I needed exactly an 80 to graduate, so I silently thanked God for small miracles. The feeling of accomplishment was fresh in the air. I went behind the red curtain with my classmates as people filed into the auditorium. I had butterflies in my stomach all over again. I had put in a lot of work to get where I was. The journey was never easy and that made me respect it even more. The ceremony couldn't have been better. Ms. Patterson came and sat right in the back like she usually did. She never accepted credit for anything. Her sitting in the back was her trademark. She played the background. Her help was genuine as it gets.

I listened to all the speeches and thought about the job opportunities we were going to have. Everybody on the stage had a degree, but where would it take us? Those were one of the few questions I had on my brain. The ceremony was very memorable. I remember the digital cameras and camera phone flashes going off. My family was sitting in the fifth row back from the stage. My mother had this stupid look on her face. Everybody else was smiling and was clapping loudly when I came to get my degree. She didn't even move. That hurt like hell, but I did an excellent job hiding it that day.

I had my marketing degree and was hoping that some type of job would open up in my field. I was tired of working at Foot Locker. I mean, it wasn't hard work, but it wasn't what I envisioned being my career.

* * * * *

Soon as I was about to leave for work, I heard footsteps coming near my bedroom. My younger brother, Jahiem, walked in.

"What up, young'n?" I said, giving him a handshake.

"Nothing."

"Nothing, huh?"

"It's just, Mommy being cheap wit' the money."

"What you mean?"

"She only gave me twenty dollars for my allowance," Jahiem said, pulling the money from his jeans pocket. I had to laugh. I remember when I thought twenty dollars was real money. Now, the dough I got I stacked as much as I could. You never knew when you would need it. I reached under my bed and pulled out a raggedy shoebox. I pulled out a stack of money and began counting it. Out the corner of my eye, I could see Jahiem's eyes brighten up. I peeled off four twenties and slid the shoebox back under my bed.

I'd been saving that money from working and hustling DVDs. I figured I had some serious change saved up between the two. I didn't have any bills like that. All I had was my cell phone and some credit cards. I told Jahiem to come sit down so I could holla at him.

"What up, Swift?" Jahiem said with clear nervousness.

"You been saving that money like I told you?" I asked sternly.

"Kind of," Jahiem said, breaking eye contact and looking down at the floor.

M.Q.W.

"I know it's hard, shit, I'm gr-."

I cut myself off, realizing I was cussing in front of my baby brother.

"It's cool. I'm a teenager now, can't you tell?" Jahiem said, tugging at a loose chin hair.

My baby brother was growing right before my eyes. The dude wore the same size sneakers as me.

"I know, I just don't want you to think it's cool."

"I know, man."

"Cool, I gotta go to work. Save some of this, and use the rest for whatever."

"I will," Jahiem said, stuffing the money in his oversized jeans. I grabbed my car keys and went to work before I was late. Malik was blowing up my cell phone while I was on my way to South Street. I looked at my screen and debated whether to answer it or not. After the fifth ring, I picked up the phone. I plugged in my ear piece and prepared myself.

"Yo, Swift, where you at?" Malik said, stalling for time.

He didn't even say hello. Who do you know just call somebody and start talking?

"Where you think, 'Lik, you only call me when you need something," I said in complete disgust.

"Mom said I gotta get a job, or else I gotta bounce," he said, sounding pitiful. "You gon' help me?"

I wanted to tell him to kick rocks, but I decided to help him, anyway. I was hoping he could change a little bit.

"You better be at Foot Locker on South Street at three sharp."

"I'll be there."

"Don't screw this up," I said as I slammed my phone shut. I threw my phone on the passenger seat and focused on the road.

Of course, a week after I got him the job, I got that inevitable call. That lazy bastard had played me big time. After I practically begged my boss to give him a chance he pulled this.

"So, you mean he said he was tired of working so hard?" I said, visibly pissed off.

"Yup. Mr. Morrison was looking for you, too," Yazmeen said, giving me a concerned look.

"He in the stockroom?"

"Yeah," Yazmeen said, barely audible.

I had a feeling I was taking an L. I basically put myself out there for Malik. I barreled past my co-workers at the speed of light. Once I got to the doorway, I made my way down them creaky, wooden stairs. Soon as I got near Mr. Morrison, he started complaining.

"Stephen, I thought you said that boy could be counted on," Mr. Morrison said with a raised eyebrow.

"I mean, at his last job, he wa—," I stuttered, realizing my mistake. I was hoping Mr. Morrison didn't catch on.

"He didn't have any previous work history, remember?" he said, catching right on.

"What you want me to do about it?" I said, getting mad.

"Nothing, you're fired," Mr. Morrison said.

"Just like that, huh? After everything I did for this store? Who's number one in sales? Me. Who covered for you? Me." I poked my chest with my index finger for emphasis.

"I'd appreciate it if you didn't show your face around here again," Mr. Morrison said as he handed me my last paycheck.

I snatched my check and jumped the steps two at a time. My co-workers acted like they weren't eavesdropping. I was pissed off that Malik had blown the opportunity. Mr. Morrison was acting like I didn't hold the store down. I wanted to break his neck. I made it to the front door like lightning. I just wanted to get as far away from the store as I could.

When I opened the door, all I could say was wow. I did

a quick assessment as I held the door open. The woman was about 5'4 and gorgeous. Her skin was copper and her silky hair fell just past her shoulders. Her business suit showcased her Coke bottle figure. I had to control myself right quick. She just screamed sophistication. She was bad, but I was on a mission. If it was meant to be, I would definitely see her again.

I was so heated that I didn't even feel like going home. I actually was free, seeing as though I was jobless. I decided to walk up South Street to Tower Records. I walked a couple blocks and went through the door as an elderly man held it for me. I went straight to the back to the magazine section. I grabbed *Maxim*, *XXL*, *The Source*, and *Vibe*. The thing I liked was nobody bothered me.

The store was busy for a Wednesday afternoon.

A magazine ad caught my eye. It was for CD inserts. I hated printing them at home. I wanted to print them in bulk. I was doing the math in my head and it would be more profitable to go with them. I logged the number in my phone and put the magazines back on the rack.

After I was done perusing that section, I went downstairs and looked through the DVD section. They had a couple deals, so I grabbed a few of them. I loved collecting DVDs. Some of the DVDs I had were still in plastic. I had every classic you could think of. Sometimes, I burned them and resold the real DVDs. I had my account with Netflix solely for that reason. I burned those DVDs religiously. I went back upstairs to pay for my items.

The only thing left to get was some blank CDs and DVDs. I damn sure wasn't getting them from Tower. I looked at the labels that read 24.99 and started cracking up. People probably thought I was crazy.

I was third in line and used that time to read the track listing of the CDs in the "New This Week" section. When I looked up, a customer was walking off with their bags. I got up to the front and placed my things on the counter. She looked like she didn't want to be there. I couldn't sympathize because I didn't have a job to not want to be at. I even smirked as I handed her the two twenty dollar bills. She took them. She sucked her teeth, and hit the button opening the cash register. She put my change on the counter instead of giving it to me. I scooped it up and rolled out. All I could do was laugh at her immaturity.

I had to park two blocks away and wasn't thrilled about it. I threw the bag in the back seat, drove a couple blocks and made the left to get to Commerce Bank near 2nd Street. I could see the line was long as hell. I got in it reluctantly. How the hell could there be one teller? I was heated. After about fifteen minutes of waiting, I got up to the counter.

I deposited half of my check into my checking and savings accounts. I grabbed my receipt and went back outside. Since it was relatively early I decided to go back home.

When I got around my way, I scanned the block looking for my mother's car. When I spotted it, I went and parked my car around back. My brake light wasn't on and it didn't surprise me. I had to put that on my list of many things to do. That was number two behind finding a job.

I grabbed the bag from the backseat, went through the garage door, and then to my room door. Soon as I went through the door it was pure chaos. There were beer cans and ashtrays on the floor. There was a fold up plastic chair and a porno was playing on the TV. I muted the TV and stepped over all the debris. My dresser drawers were open; all clothes were scattered on the bed. I knew that my brother was the culprit. My closet was empty. All my NBA jerseys and hats were gone. All that was left were hangers. Luckily, he couldn't fit my shoes. I moved the bed and checked for my money box which was still there.

I began to clean up my room. I went up stairs and got air freshener, a broom, and some trash bags. I swept up all the cigarette butts and blunt ashes. I grabbed all the bottles and threw them in the bag as well. I snatched the sheets off my bed and threw them in the dirty clothes hamper. I put fresh sheets on the bed and sprayed the room with the air freshener. I got it together quickly before I called Block up.

"What's good?"

"You busy?"

"Naw. I was just going over some stocks I had. You aight?"

"Naw, man. It's Malik."

"He stealin' your stuff again?"

"Yeah. I came home, dawg, and everything was chaotic, like he was on some crack head type jawn."

"I ain't wanna tell you, baby boy, but Andre saw him up top coppin'."

"Coppin' what?" I asked, getting a little worried.

"I'm thinking it was Lean."

"That cough syrup crap?"

"Yeah," Block said.

I was immediately pissed off. He probably was high off that stuff. Pops told me a couple times he came home and he was sleep on the steps. It broke my heart to see my brother going through that. It was something that he brought on himself. I already gave him that speech and he chose not to follow my advice. There wasn't much more I could do. I honestly tried everything in my power.

"Can you come scoop me?"

"No doubt. When you gone be ready?"

"Give me a half."

"Aight, I'm a text when I get close."

"Cool. One."

"One."

I took a shower and got dressed in the meantime. I had to at least take two showers a day. Hygiene was one thing I never played with. After I was fully dressed, I sprayed on some cologne. I looked in the mirror and made sure I was straight. While I was waiting for Block, I turned on Eddie Murphy's *Raw*.

Soon as he got to my favorite part, I got Block's text.

Block hit the button to unlock the door and I hopped in the passenger seat.

"I was so heated I forgot to tell you."

"What?" Block said, turning the corner.

"You know I got fired today, right?"

"Man, stop playing."

"Real talk."

"For what?"

I just gave him that look.

"Malik again?"

"You know it."

"Ya parents need to put homie out. I mean, damn, how you get him a job and now you don't got one. That's crazy."

"That's the even better part."

"There's more?"

"Yup."

"Go 'head," Block said, shaking his head.

"He quit. Soon as he played my manager, he played me. He quit on the busiest day we ever had. Ain't that ironic? He gave me my last check and everything. I ain't gon' lie, dawg, I was real salty."

"You need anything, you let me know."

"Thanks, man."

As Block drove, we listened to a jazz radio station; I didn't recognize the artist. I was feeling the saxophone part though. Block was talking to somebody about real estate and I was left to think of the day's events. All I could do was smile.

I had spent so much energy on being angry. I didn't know where we were going, and honestly, I didn't care. I just needed something to take my mind of things.

Block got off the phone by the time we pulled into a parking spot. He killed the engine and we hopped out. The street was unusually dark. I followed Block's lead and we ended up in front of a building that looked like an abandoned warehouse. Block knocked on the black door and we waited for it to be answered. A slot opened quickly then closed. I heard the locks being opened and then the door. A 6'7 bald, black dude opened the door and proceeded to pat us down. Block handed him a fifty and gave him dap.

He opened another door and the music was deafening. There was a small bar to our left. Directly next to the bar, a fully nude girl was gyrating for the customers. When she bent over exposing everything, they threw money at her and banged on the bar. They hollered and clapped until her set was over. Block ordered his drink and then tapped me. I had to close my mouth. Most of the women only had stilettos on.

"What you drinking?"

"Huh?"

"You thirsty?"

"Oh yeah," I replied. "Can I get a coke with no ice?"

After a few moments, the bartender put my drink on a napkin. She put two red straws in it and attended to the other patrons.

One of the strippers came and sat at the bar on the stool next to me. She had to be the thickest girl I had ever seen. I still couldn't believe that she was fully nude. She smelled just like lavender. When she put her hand in my lap, my mind went blank. All the problems I had evaporated. She led me to the backroom through the crowd into the private rooms. Before I went in, I saw Block raise his glass. He damn sure knew how to cheer me up.

Chapter 6
Block

Block and Swift walked to the champagne-colored Jaguar and got in. Block hit the button and dropped the top. In no time, Block was turning down Market Street in search of a parking lot.

"You think I should have shot my dad?" Block said, not taking his eyes off the road. He knew he caught Swift off guard. That question had been haunting him for a long time. He trusted Swift and was confident he would keep it one hundred.

"If he put his hands on your mother," Swift replied, "he deserved it."

"Would you have done the same?"

He could see Swift's mind spinning when he asked him that.

"As a man, I would holla at my pops. I don't think I could shoot him though. He would have to do something extra extreme."

"Far as I'm concerned, he was just a sperm donor," Block said, smirking. They both shared a laugh.

Swift decided to change the subject. "I see you got a new watch, playboy."

"Oh yeah, I copped it not too long ago. I get up there right, and guess what the saleswoman told me?"

"What?"

"Sir, we have a wonderful payment plan," Block said in a woman's voice. "I threw five stacks on the counter and watched her jaw drop. I guess she figured since I wasn't as sharp that day, I couldn't afford it."

They finally pulled up to a parking garage and found a spot. Block must have circled the parking lot at least three times before parking. They walked up 10th and Market to Sneaker Villa looking crisp. They were getting extended stares until they walked into the store.

"Sweetheart, pass me that black Nets hat," Block told the female cashier. She was wearing a Braves hat with her brown micro braids hanging to her shoulders.

"What size?"

"Seven and a half." While she was searching for the hat, he got a glimpse of her thickness. It looked like her jeans were drawn on. She smiled and handed him the hat.

"As a matter fact, give me them thirty hats on that rack right there," Block said, counting crisp hundred dollar bills.

"All of these?" she said, jocking.

"Yeah, all them, baby girl," he said smoothly.

He checked on Swift and found him trying on black suede trees. When Swift got up to walk, some dude bumped him. Block saw the dude put his hand in Swift's face, and instantly, it was a problem. He walked over to them with the immediate ice grill.

"We got a problem, fam?" Block said, removing his glasses and moving Swift out the way.

"Yeah, your man a little too clumsy, homie," the guy spat.

He was tall and stocky. Block had lost a couple fights, but his gun still had a perfect record.

"Really," Block said as he pulled the .40 Cal quickly from his waist. He was ready to off him right there in the middle

M.Q.W.

of Sneaker Villa.

"You got it," the dude said. "I'll see you again, you can bet on it." He put his hands up and left. Block put his gun away and his glasses back on. He'd been in war plenty of times before. When he saw that dude again, he'd definitely handle that.

"You aight?" Block said, grabbing Swift's shoulder playfully.

"Yeah, I'm straight."

Block totally forgot they were in public. Nobody was that shocked in the store. A few people left in the middle of the altercation. The skinny, acne faced manager told Swift and Block to bounce. Swift grabbed his trees, put them on, and put his week old Nikes in the Timberland box. Swift and Block put their money on the counter for their stuff and walked out the store.

The minute they left, onlookers were being nosy. As they were going back toward the car, Block's phone vibrated. He immediately became agitated. He knew what it was already.

"Speak."

"Slim came short with the count again, plus, I saw him down Jewelers Row copping watches."

"Handle it, not now, right now," Block ordered before stuffing his phone into his pants pocket.

* * * * *

"Ain't that Block right there?" Thoro said, pointing out the driver side window.

"Damn, sure is," Speed said, grabbing his cell phone. He dialed Bird's number. After a few rings, Bird picked up.

"What you want us to do? We got Block right in our line of sight," Speed said, hoping to get a chance to bust his gun.

"Just keep eyes on him for now."

"Aight."

Speed closed his phone a little disappointed. He knew not to voice his opinion, but he also couldn't deny his feelings about Block. His and Thoro's cuts were getting lighter because of Block taking over their boss' corners. He just hoped that Bird's plan to fall back worked.

* * * * *

Later that night, Trill and Stack rode in a black Honda Accord. They drove up Washington Ave. and turned on Tasker.

Trill killed the lights. He cut the engine, hit the AC, and turned the station to 510 AM. The guns and clips slid out backwards from the stash spot. He passed a gun and clip to Stack. The loading and cocking sounds of the guns caused the two killers to smile.

There wasn't anybody outside. The street lamp blinked on and off, giving off very little light. They crept up to the house quiet as mimes.

Trill zipped up his black hoodie and pulled his skully over his ears. Stack was right behind him as they approached the door. Trill knocked on the flimsy white screen door with the barrel of the .45.

The rattle of the screen door brought Slim to the door.

"Who that?" he asked.

At the sight of the two pistols, he dropped the beer bottle, which shattered on the cement steps. Slim used that split second to push Trill into Stack, causing Stack's gun to slide into the street. Trill, now seeing the back of Slim's wife-beater tee, squeezed the trigger, putting a hole in the arm of the sofa.

"You like to rob people, huh?" The bass in Trill's voice caused Slim to jump back, holding his hands near his face.

"I got the money plus interest!" Slim screamed in

desperation.

"Where it at? Don't play me, either. I won't hesitate to blow ya head off."

Slim led them down the stairs, walking slowly. The moment he ducked, bullets began to tear through the wooden stairs and banister, cracking them both. Trill and Stack both blindly shot back. While the unknown men took cover, Trill and Stack ran to the opposite corner.

Stack mistimed it when he went to shoot again. Two bullets pierced his chest, sending him to the ground back first. Soon as Trill saw Stack hit the ground, he quickly emptied his clip and took cover. While they were returning bullets, Trill stuffed a fresh clip in his gun and slid the top back.

The shooters' bullets were taking chunks out of the wall above where Trill and Stack were situated. Trill unexpectedly popped up and put one shot into each of their foreheads. Their bodies made a huge thud in the quiet basement.

He put his gun away and noticed Stack wincing. Stack tore his vest off and rubbed his chest. There were dark red bruises just below his collarbone. Trill helped him up off the ground; they had one more thing to take care of.

They searched for Slim and thought he escaped during the commotion. Then, they heard the moron's cell phone. A ringtone blared until they found his location. Trill knocked on the laundry room door until he heard Slim move around behind the door.

"Slim, if you ain't out here in thirty seconds, I'ma blow this door off the hinges," Trill said calmly.

"C'mon, dawg, you know we still cool. What we gotta do to make this right?" Slim said, unlocking the door.

"Trill, go start the car up while I handle this," Stack said barely above a whisper. Stack never said much but when he did, it meant one of two things, you were family or you were in trouble.

"Aight," Trill said as he coasted out the basement door. He got to the car, started it up, and drove around back. Minutes later, Stack came running out of the door holding his gun by his side. Trill pulled off leaving tire marks.

When the cops found Slim, his eyeballs were removed, and his neck had been cut to the bone. Bullet holes were scattered throughout his lifeless body.

Chapter 7
Swift

I was exhausted from going up and down the Broad Street line looking for employment. Sometimes, it was easier for me to ride the bus. My bus pass was way cheaper than my monthly gas bill.

Keon was the one who taught me job interview etiquette. I wore a tie, made sure I looked them in the eye, and enunciated every word. Everyday my mother would ask did I have a job yet. She knew I didn't have one, but she insisted on aggravating me.

That was the same reason Keon left home at eighteen. He and Camille got into an argument over employment. Keon told me he never wanted to hit a woman until that moment. Keon would stay out at all times of the night just to avoid her. I remember because he took me with him. Almost all his friends had Sega Genesis or Super Nintendo. All they did was play Madden, play basketball, and talk to girls. I remember riding on his handlebars. When we got home late at night, he always got in trouble. Everything my brother did, I was there with him.

When we moved with Camille, his passion for basketball died down. I didn't get to go out with him that often either. That made me angry. Sometimes, he left the crib just to leave.

When Camille caught wind of it, she confronted him.

"Where you coming from?" my mother said from the chair she'd been sitting in for the last three hours.

"None of your business," my brother mumbled a little too loud.

I snuck to the top of the steps when I heard the door click and my brother walk in. I observed the whole thing through the slits in the wooden banister.

"Boy, do you know who you're talking to?"

"Yeah, every time I come in, you question me like I'm a criminal or something."

"Well, if you don't want to be questioned, take your black ass to your own home," my mom replied with a cold tone. "I am the adult. It's my way or the highway."

"The highway it is," Keon said, grabbing his gym bag and slamming the front door. I started down the steps and stopped halfway down. My eyes connected with my mother's icy cold glare. I had ill feelings toward my mom since that day and it only worsened over the years. She put my best friend out the house. After their argument, Keon stormed out our home and didn't return until two days later. He got a surprise upon his return.

Camille had packed his remaining bags and had them sitting in the living room. On top of his suitcase was an envelope with a note and $1500 in cash. The note read:

Dear Keon,

Since you made it crystal clear you are grown, here is some money. Hopefully, you can find a place to live. I will not be disrespected in my home any longer.
Sincerely,
Camille

Every time I thought about that story, it was mind boggling. I couldn't believe that my mother would put him out on the street like a stranger.

* * * * *

I was determined to get rid of my DVD inventory. I had about 250 DVDs in a cardboard box. I had to hit my three major spots – all high traffic areas.

Bootleggers hit me up heavy when they saw the inventory I was working with. I wholesaled them half of the DVDs. I moved the other half between 52nd Street and 69th Street. I made $800 out there. Now that I had a little extra paper, I was good. I looked at my watch and noticed that it was only 2:30 p.m. I decided to grab a few more applications since I was already downtown.

I went to Rite Aid and got one from the stuck up clerk at the register. I caught the bus across the street and rode to the Gallery. It was only a few blocks away, but I had an all day pass. After a few minutes, I hopped off the bus and walked a block or so to the entrance of the Gallery. Before I could open the door, a bum was begging me for change. I saw this guy down here every time I came. With all the people that came to the mall, I knew he was holdin'. I threw him a single and went down the escalator.

Although I hated retail, I needed a job like yesterday. By the time I left the mall, I had a book bag full of applications. I hated the pressure of going home and facing my mother without a job. I was tired of hearing the story about my mother working at fifteen years old. I didn't know what it would take to convince her I wasn't her.

I had savings, sure, but I didn't want to completely blow that without additional income coming in.

Sometimes, I would stare at my degree and become

so pissed off I wanted to tear it in half. Block's voice kept echoing in my head. I knew what he did and how he got his money. I never knocked him for what he did, but it wasn't me. I mean, it's hard to fall back though when your best friend runs the city and spends money like water runs – freely. I tried to keep myself grounded and turn a blind eye to it. With all the rejection, I didn't know how long that would last.

M.Q.W.

Chapter 8
Block

Block drove to Delaware to check on his real estate projects. The space where the condominiums would sit was perfect for the downtown crowd. There were clubs, restaurants, and sports events in the vicinity. He always saw opportunity when he went out there. The city moved at a slow pace and it was the perfect time to put some juice into it. It was a great starting place. It was relativity quiet on the real estate front, so he decided a long time ago to jump on it. It was already paying huge dividends.

He sat in his truck and looked at the water off in the distance. The view was beautiful and it was one of the rare instances of relaxation taken advantage of by Block. He was always quiet about his dirt. A lot of the dudes he saw when he came up were too loud for his liking. People mistook that as a weakness. For Block, it was an asset. He never got caught up in telling somebody what he was going to do. He was too busy doing it. He had seen, on several occasions, how the cops had those magical raids and came away with the whole stash and all the money. He never kept drugs where he stayed. His rules were strict. That was the reason he had survived for so long in this game.

The less people knew about his business endeavors the

better. That's why it was so important to have Swift around. Swift was one of the few people that he had complete trust in. That was a short list of individuals. His lawyers always checked the paperwork that he received. He knew it was legit, but he wanted a second and third opinion.

He cruised the city of Wilmington with the AC on max. He looked out the windows at the people that hustled up and down the streets. He went back to the times he made trips back and forth between Wilmington and Philly on the R2 train. The thought made him smile. He had put in much work in those very streets. A part of him would be forever tied down there. He flew past King Street and made a left to get to the parking deck which was a block away. He pulled into the entrance and grabbed the ticket from the machine. He parked on the 3rd floor, which was on the roof. He made sure he grabbed everything before he locked the car up and made his way back down to the street level.

He had a few meetings with the city's higher ups. People had to be bribed left and right. Before they jumped off the bridge, they wanted financial security. He knew it all was a part of the game. He had no problem securing his plans. He gamed any and everybody to get his projects green lighted.

Block was dressed for the occasion. He breathed style since the day he was born. His black Roberto Cavalli suit and Hermes briefcase made him fit right into the day time business crowd that walked the downtown area. Once he got up to the 10th floor of the building, he straightened himself up.

When he did walk in, he had the confidence and swagger that couldn't be ignored. Everyone at the conference table acknowledged the young man with firm handshakes. By the time he finished, he had the whole room intrigued.

* * * * *

Pump emerged from the shadows with gun in hand. He hated how cocky Block was. He set out to prove that he could be touched like any other dude in the streets. It wasn't business with him; it was personal. He was accompanied by his right hand man, Blaze. The men wore stone faces as they peered across the street at the abandoned trap house that housed Block's packages.

Pump took one last drag and flicked his cigarette onto the curb. He peeped Trill vacate the block. That made the task that much easier. When Stack saw the figures approaching, it was too late.

Pump raised his weapon and gave strict instructions. "Walk ya monkey ass to the door and get 'em to open it, fam."

Stack couldn't reach his gun that was close by. It was located on the tire of his parked Escalade. He cursed himself for slipping up. Stack knocked on the door three times before a young boy answered.

At the sight of the unkempt beard and maroon do-rag, he knew what time it was. Soon as he tried to run, Pump put a bullet just left of the boy's head. The bullet put a baseball-sized hole in the wall.

"Get on the floor wit' y'all hands on y'all heads," Pump said while pulling his second handgun. Blaze watched his partner's back as he conducted business. This was routine for Pump. The dealers in the city knew about his exploits, but never knew when he would strike. That's the part he loved. He wasn't biased. He robbed any and everybody who had money.

"Where it at?" he asked the young boy who opened the door.

"What you talking 'bout?"

Pump leveled both guns and put a shot into each of the boy's kneecaps. He howled in pain as he held his legs.

"Need I rephrase the question?" Pump asked.

"Upstairs bathroom," the boy said through clenched teeth.

Pump sent Blaze to retrieve the drug stash. After a few moments, Blaze threw the brown paper bag down the steps. Pump caught the bag and put it in his jacket pocket.

"Nice doing business with y'all. Oh, and tell Block I said holla at me," Pump said, laughing hysterically as he and Blaze walked out the door.

* * * * *

Trill was third behind an overweight couple who seemed to be ordering everything that was displayed above the counter. He kept glancing at his watch ever so often. Block had a strict rule about his captains not being at their post. He knew he was pushing it. He just hoped that everything was still all good when he got back.

He finally got to the front and pulled out the paper that everybody wrote their orders on. He read the list and paid for the food. He stood off to the side waiting for them to bring his food out. After about ten minutes, he grabbed the bags and made the walk back to the traphouse. Using his long legs, which got him places in half the time as a normal human being, something didn't feel right. He shoved a handful of French fries in his mouth absentmindedly. Snapping back to reality, he patted his waist, making sure his gun was still there. Feeling the weight of his .45 pistol, he felt relived.

As he was waiting for the light to change, he saw a white van zoom by. It definitely looked out of place. He dropped the bags, pulled his gun, and ran as fast as he could back to the spot. He noticed the door wide open when he got close enough. He put his head down, knowing he had screwed up. Trill was always on point and this was one of his rare mistakes. When he saw the familiar faces, he put his gun back on his waist. He saw one of the young boys bleeding and ordered one of the soldiers to get him to the hospital.

"What the hell happened?" Trill asked, viewing the gaping hole in the wall. "Pump robbed us, didn't he?" Trill said, answering his own question.

Everybody just nodded. There had to be retaliation for what Pump did. The problem was that he moved around so much you could never put a finger on him. Trill knew that he had to face Block sooner or later. He kept it "G" and pulled out his phone and dialed Block's number. Soon as Block answered, he took a deep breath and prepared himself.

CHAPTER 9
BLOCK

Block wanted Swift's birthday to be a memorable event. He had several things to set up for it to go smoothly. After cutting down his list of hotels, he chose the penthouse suite at the Omni Hotel as the backdrop. He drove downtown to the hotel to make the reservations. He found a parking spot down the street and made long strides toward the entrance of the hotel. His walk was authentic. It was one of confidence. When people were in Block's presence, they gravitated toward him. He stepped up to counter and waited for the hotel attendant to finish up with her call. The slender, white woman got off the phone and turned toward Block with a smile that seemed like it was filled with fluorescent light bulbs.

"How may we accommodate you today?"

"I need the penthouse suite."

She ran her freshly manicured finger down a list of the occupancies. She stopped and her facial expression changed. She looked up at the handsome young man and was thinking of something better to say. She opted for the truth. After all, she valued her job a whole hell of a lot.

"I'm sorry, sir, we are nearing full capacity. I have a few wonderful rooms that I would be happy to set you up with."

Block just smiled. The same smile that made woman's panties instantly wet.

"I think y'all just had a cancelation."

"Excuse me, sir?" the attendant said, confused.

Block didn't speak another word. He pulled out a stack of hundred dollar bills and sat it on the counter. It looked as if she wanted to say something, but her mouth wouldn't respond to her brain's commands.

"Half that's yours," Block said before walking off. Before he got outside he asked one more question. "We have an understanding, correct?"

She just nodded numbly. She had never seen that much money at one time. It had to be at least three months of her pay staring her in the face. She scooped the money up and counted it. She quickly got on the phone and got off just as fast. He smiled as he got back outside. He knew that money talked. It was nothing to Block. He blew that on dress socks.

When he was coming outside, he saw a patrolman putting a ticket on his windshield. When the patrolman turned to see who was walking across the street, he snatched the ticket back off the windshield. He caught Block's ice cold smile and almost pissed on himself. He quickly hustled around the corner to avoid confrontation.

Block got to his next destination in Northeast Philly. He drove through the quiet community, scanning the houses, looking for familiarity. He spotted the house ten minutes into his drive. He slowed down and turned into the cul-de-sac. The Mexican gardeners were making sure that the front looked impeccable. Soon as Block stepped up toward the extravagant home, the aroma of fresh cut grass clogged his nose. He parked the Maybach behind a cherry red Ferrari Spider. Block adjusted the gun in his waist, knocked on the door twice, and took a step back.

Joseph answered the door like they were in Miami. He had

on a white terry cloth robe with blue swimming trunks. Thin, gold jewelry adorned his wrist and neck. He was wearing black and gold Yves Saint Laurent glasses.

"Block, come on in," Joseph said, opening the door so Block could see the women he had assembled.

When Block stepped inside the foyer, he rubbed his hands together. They were standing one after the other on the staircase. He walked up on them closer, examining them. They were all sorts of shades, sizes, and colors. He saw a couple that he would like to put work in with.

"How much I owe you?"

"Twenty, plus five, for me of course," Joseph said without hesitation.

"Aight," Block said, reaching in his left pocket pulling out a rubber banded stack of money. He tossed the money to Joey. "Have the women at the Omni around 8 p.m. Not a minute less. I ain't playing, Joe."

"I got you, baby."

"Aight," Block said, walking off. Block really couldn't stand Joey. He was a scumbag, but had access to the best women Philly had to offer. That alone made him at least usable.

On the way back to his condo, Block phoned his boys and told them to meet him at his condo in Center City. After a few minutes of waiting, he saw Trill and Stack pull into the parking garage. They came out and approached the car. They knew he was still pissed off about the other night. He said his peace and told Trill he had to be smarter next time.

They switched seats and Trill drove the Maybach. Stack got in the car and they pulled off. In the meantime, Block went over some real estate info on his laptop. That was what really made Block happy. He was far smarter than people gave him credit for. His street legend overshadowed his other talents.

"Yo, Trill, throw something in," Block said, passing him

a stack of CDs. Trill picked some R&B, a change of pace for him and Stack who usually listened to Hip Hop.

"Turn off Spruce," Block said as they were getting closer.

Swift's mother was sitting on the steps when they got out the car. When they approached the stairs, she greeted them all with love.

"Where Swift at?" Block asked after hugging Swift's mother.

"He's down in the basement on that damn laptop," Camille said flatly.

When they entered the cozy living space, they spotted Swift's dad. He was on the couch watching television.

"How you, old-timer?" Block said, fake boxing him. After they exchanged a brother-like hug, they all engaged in small talk.

"I haven't seen you gentlemen in a long time. How y'all been doing?" he asked.

"We been getting paper," they all said, flashing watches that were flooded with tic-tac sized diamonds.

"Me too," Swift's dad said, flashing his butterscotch Audemars Piguet watch. It was like Swift's dad was always in the loop. He wasn't an old head trying too hard to be young. He just had that undeniable swagger. It came to him naturally, and he never forced it. His Ralph Lauren button up was crisp as usual. Block respected the older gentleman who was still young at heart. Block knew Swift's dad still had people in the game getting paper for him.

They all walked down the stairs that led to Swift's room. Block knocked three times, paused, and knocked again. It was the same cadence from high school. Swift knew the sound and immediately unlocked his door and let them in.

"What, you a hermit now?" Block said, laughing.

"You know me. I always got a hustle lined up."

"What your peoples get you for your birthday?" Block asked curiously.

"Pops gave me some paper and this joint right here," Swift said, clicking away on his laptop.

"What did your moms get you?" Trill asked sarcastically.

Swift gave him a "You can't be serious" look.

"Nothing," Swift said in an icy, cold tone. "That woman doesn't even act like I'm celebrating my birthday."

Block hated how Swift and his mother's relationship had soured over the years. All they really had to do was talk about it. The problem was they were both stubborn.

"Y'all ready to go?" Swift said, already halfway out his room.

"Yeah, first stop is the liquor store," Block said, walking out the room behind Trill and Stack.

Swift walked right by his mother without even acknowledging her presence. Before he got in the car, he gave her one more look of disgust. Block caught the whole episode and could only shake his head. He always wanted to call Swift on it, but he didn't want him to think he was taking sides.

The four young men cruised the streets of Philly. Each was in his own zone. Block was putting figures together on the laptop. He looked over and saw that distant look in his friend's eyes. Today, they were having a celebration and Block would be damned if Swift threw it away for his mother's sake. Block vowed to show Swift a good time.

Chapter 10
Swift

We copped several cases of liquor from the beer distributor. We had enough for twelve damn parties. We got everything from Hypnotic to Crown Royal. Block made the phone calls and set up the entertainment for the night. When I saw the signs for New Jersey, I got confused.

"Yo, Block, where we going?" I said with a raised eyebrow.

"Handle somethin'," Block said, looking in the rearview mirror at Trill and Stack who were now smirking. I was about to snap. Then, we turned and I saw a car dealership up ahead. When we got onto the lot, my jaw dropped to the floor. The lot showcased Jaguars, BMWs, and Bentleys. Before I could speak, Block did.

"You might wanna holla at my man, L, over there."

I approached the salesman as cool as possible.

"Swift?" L said.

"Yeah."

"Follow me."

When we walked a few feet, we were standing in front of a porcelain white 760 Benz. I saw the navigation system and headrest TV screens playing a DVD. The guts were cappuccino and the seats were leather. I grabbed the keys from L and peeled off behind Block. The looks I was getting made me feel like a king.

As soon as we all arrived at the Omni, Trill started hitting on the desk clerks. He was acting like it wasn't a room full of girls upstairs.

Block, Trill, and Stack went ahead while I waited for Keon and Jalen. Soon as they showed up, we boarded the elevator. We got to the floor and made the long walk to the suite. I knocked on the door twice and Block opened the door, allowing us to pass through. Soon as the door opened we were greeted by the smell of Buffalo wings. There was a long table filled with more finger foods and bottles of alcohol. Block handed each of us a bottle of Krug Rose.

Everything in the room looked expensive. It seemed like nothing was supposed to be touched. The drapes over the windows were thick and gave a slight view of Center City. The wallpaper was decorated with gold and white stripes. The carpet was spotless and a chandelier hung directly in the middle of the ceiling.

There were nine girls for our entertainment. There were all types of chicks in there. The first chick that caught my eye was unbelievable. She was 5'9 with olive-colored skin and 38FF breasts.

The girls put enough chairs out so all the men could sit down. When they sat my chair down, it was a throne. It was trimmed in gold with blue suede covering the seat. They put the stereo on playing *The Best of R. Kelly* CD. The girls left for a moment, leaving us to salivate. The room was going wild with anticipation. I had no clue what the hell was going down. The lights went off and it was completely dark. A spotlight came on, shining brightly on them when they walked out.

Every one of them was voluptuous and their perfume mixture floated through the air. All nine girls came out behind each other. They were facing away from us at first. When R.

Kelly began crooning again, they turned toward us one by one. They blew kisses at us with a wave of the hand. They all had pinstriped suits with matching hats. They covered their eyes. It made things mysterious, which was right up my alley. I took a few more swigs of the pink champagne, enjoying the taste.

They gyrated and rubbed on themselves with their eyes closed. After the song switched, they tore of their clothes. That left them in nothing but matching bras, panties, and stilettos. When they were sure they had our full attention, they began to give us thorough lap dances. They shortened the spotlight and put it directly on me and the first chick I saw. She was so close I could smell the strong scent of spearmint on her breath. Her breasts were rubbing against me while she danced in front of me. She grabbed my head, putting it between her mounds. I tried to grab them and she smacked my hand, waving her index finger. She sat on my lap and looked back at me with the sexiest stare I'd ever seen.

She snaked her body all the way to the ground, trailing kisses along my jeans. The material from my jeans rose the moment she kissed near my zipper. For her finale, she dry humped me and bit on my right ear. Her hair smelled good and body smelled even better. I kept drinking the Krug Rose, letting the night's events play out. I was feeling extra horny. That, mixed with the lap dance, was too much. I motioned for her to get up so we could finish in the bedroom. All the men started to howl when she took my hand and led me to the bed room.

"So you're Swift, huh?" she said, tossing her bra to the ground.

"Yeah, I'm Sw—" I couldn't even finish my sentence before she was unbuckling my jeans. She pulled my boxers and jeans down to my ankles, then completely off. I wasn't usually bold, but I started roughly kissing her and grabbing her all over. She pushed me back on the bed and stared at me with her hand on her hip. She grabbed a condom out the drawer and tore the wrapping off. She walked over, got on her knees, and put the condom on me with her mouth.

She positioned herself on top and was riding me so hard the bed was jumping off the ground. I grabbed her around her thick waist, controlling the rhythm. I flipped her, picked her up, and spun her around. She really surprised me when she had two more girls come in the room. Those girls weren't shy at all. They were kissing on each other and everything. They did any and everything I asked. Block definitely got his money's worth with them.

I got a couple more lap dances and was ready to bounce. I was beginning to get tired. I wobbled to the door, not able to stand. I handed Jalen my keys. I needed someone to make sure I could get home safe. It was really the first time I got drunk.

"Ay, Swift, you leaving already?" Block said, now clutching a gold bottle of champagne.

"Yeah, I got an early start tomorrow."

Block snapped his fingers and the two girls at his sides instantly unsnapped their bras. I didn't recognize them from the first batch of women. Their voluptuous breasts didn't drop at all. They were staring straight at me, inviting me to touch.

"You sure you wanna leave all this?" he said, looking at both of them, then back at me.

It took every ounce of willpower to leave at that point.

"Naw, I'm a get up with you later though," I said, looking over both of their bodies one last time.

I gave Block dap and then routed with Jalen. We took the elevator downstairs and got the car. I dragged myself in the seat, and we drove up Chestnut Street.

It was definitely a day to remember. On top of getting the wheel I wanted, Block really threw me off with the party. I was expecting some chill type affair. The night also made me realize the life that Block lived. I knew the car was like sixty Gs easy. I wanted that type of paper, but I knew with that type of paper came different types of headaches. I wasn't sure I was ready for it, but the dressings, I had to admit, made me think about joining forces with Block.

CHAPTER 11
BLOCK

Block sat on the edge of his California King sized bed, blowing cigar smoke into the air. Smoking always calmed him when he was stressed. His empire was growing by the day. It was getting harder to keep his eyes everywhere. He pressed a button on a painting of himself that opened a private doorway.

He had his house custom detailed when he moved in. It was the spot where he felt safe. The opening had a reinforced steel door that led to Block's personal chambers. The lock was pass code verified. His millions were stashed in three six-foot safes along with bags of E pills.

To say that Block was leery of people would be an understatement. He had to bust his gun on several occasions. It could be a stick up kid, a new jack, or a rival dealer who tried him. He trusted a select few and anybody else could get it. The house was his one safe haven. When he went there, he didn't worry about his street beef or any other issues. Here he could clear his mind and concentrate on his real estate ventures.

He filled up a duffle bag with money and tucked his weapon. To the right of the safes was an elevator. He pressed the button and waited for the silver doors to open. Once they did, he rode it to the basement level. He looked through his extensive car choices before choosing a gray Audi S8.

Block threw the bag of money in the trunk and put his gun under his seat. He zoomed toward the 55th Street Precinct. Block hated doing this, but it had to be done. He drove down Pine Street and parked across the street. He saw a shorty posted up and approached him. Block handed him a hundred dollar bill and told him what to do. The boy went into the station and handed the desk officer the bag.

"What is this, young man?" the officer inquired.

"Payment," the boy said before walking off.

The officer unzipped the bag and nearly choked on his turkey sandwich. He immediately picked up the phone and dialed a number.

* * * * *

Block was a little hungry, so he made the drive completely across town to get to Penrose Diner in South Philly. He got there in twenty minutes, speeding as he usually did. He parked the car and swiftly made his way toward the entrance. He pulled out some change and got the *Daily News* from the machine. He loved the diner because he could get away and enjoy a meal without being bothered. He needed peace and quiet every now and again.

The atmosphere was lively. The waitresses whizzed by, barely holding on to the multiple plates they were balancing. Block took a seat in the far left corner of the establishment and began reading his newspaper. A waiter came with her pen and pad, ready to take his order. When Block saw her, he closed the newspaper and put it down. She gave a smile which he returned. She was attractive. He knew she was a college girl. Probably in her freshman year.

"Can I start you off with a beverage?" she asked, revealing the dimples on both sides of her cheeks.

M.Q.W.

"Yes, I'd like a coffee, and can you bring extra cream as well?"

"Ok. I'll be right back."

As she walked off to the kitchen, he saw how thick she really was. She had to be maybe 5'3, and one hundred and sixty pounds of pure beauty. He definitely had to scoop that.

She came back and set a cup down, and poured the steaming hot coffee. She set the plate of creamers and grabbed the sugar from the next table.

She swept the hair out of her eye and asked Block, "Are you ready to order?"

"Yeah, I'll have the T-bone steak and cheese eggs."

"Alright," she said like a shy schoolgirl. She nearly bumped into another waiter walking back to the kitchen.

Block picked up the newspaper and started back where he had stopped. He flipped it over, noticing the Sixers had lost again. That meant that he had lost $1,000. No matter how many times they lost, he still put his money on them. He fell in love with them the first year away at school. He and Swift used to listen to the games on whatever radio they could find.

Just as he was in mid thought, the waiter came back with Block's food. The aroma was unbelievable. He had to do everything in his power not to snatch the food out of her hands. She set the food down and absently wiped her hands on her apron.

"Do you need anything else?"

"No, thank you, sweetheart."

Block sat and enjoyed the tender steak and perfectly scrambled eggs. He went to sip his coffee and noticed that it was empty. He waited for his waitress to come into view and waved her over.

"Can I get some more coffee, please?"

"Sure thing."

She went and retrieved the coffee pot and refilled the empty cup with a wide smile on her face.

He finished off his food and drank the last sip of his coffee before grabbing his newspaper. He wrote his number on a napkin and covered it with the fifty dollar bill. He took one more look at the beautiful woman before exiting the diner.

He got to the Maybach and started the engine. Teena Marie and Rick James came blasting through the speakers. He backed out the spot and drove out the parking lot. Soon as he pulled out, a car slowly started to follow the Maybach.

* * * * *

"Everybody on the floor now," Mav screamed, waving a P95. He was in the process of robbing WSFS Bank on Market Street in Delaware. He was a two-time loser on his way to his third strike. The startled bank employees did exactly as they were told. That was, until the inevitable happened. A brave security guard aimed his gun at Mav.

"Put the gun down slowly, sir," the security guard said in an authoritative tone.

"Really?" Mav said with laughter. He put a bullet in the hand of the security guard, causing him to drop his gun. The officer went down in pain. The crowd gasped.

"Now, try me again, and I'ma blow your other hand off," Mav screamed, tightening the grip on his gun. "Let this idiot be an example to all y'all heroes."

Mav threw a bag on the counter and gave the teller a "hurry up" look. She quickly shoveled large stacks of bills into the black bag. At the same time, she was pressing a hidden button. Mav caught wind of her quick hand movements and put a bullet in her forehead.

"This ain't enough," Mav screamed.

Mav waved another employee over to retrieve the money.

80 M.Q.W.

The male employee quickly ran into the chamber with the bag. He came back with the bag stuffed. Mav snatched the bag and looked at the money with excitement. He zipped the bag up and ran out the exit.

He could see the cops approaching as he ran. He made a right and almost got hit as he ran across the street. The crowd at Rodney Square gasped as Mav ran by them with a bag of money and a handgun. He could hear someone shouting through a bullhorn. He put a couple of stacks in his jeans and threw the rest into the air. The crowd immediately went crazy over the money. People were trampling over one another to get to it.

The cop cars flooded the area, surrounding Mav and the crowd of people.

"Put your weapon down now," a police officer yelled.

The officer pulled his weapon and approached the crowd. The clothes matched, but the face didn't. A Mexican man in Mav's jacket smiled up at the officer. The officer didn't care for the arrest; he just wanted the spotlight and attention he knew it would lead to. Amongst the confusion, Mav made his way to a store to switch clothes. He dumped his gun in a nearby alleyway. He walked in casually and haphazardly searched through the clothes racks. An overly happy sales associate approached him.

"How are you, sir? Can I interest you in any of our fine suits today?"

"Yeah, I need something real fast…and sharp." Even in the heat of the battle, Mav craved being fresh. After getting his measurements, the associate had Mav hooked up. Mav paid and walked out the store as normal as he could. He looked so harmless, the approaching police officers didn't even give him a second look.

Chapter 12
Swift

It seems Camille came home early to surprise Pops and ended up being the one surprised. She caught Pops and another woman in bed. I got every detail I could from one of the officers. I was only gone for twenty four hours and couldn't believe the turn of events.

The officers escorted Pops to the back of the squad car. When that car door slammed, my heart sunk to my stomach. I looked at my mother and saw her eyes were red and swollen.

"Where they taking Pops?"

"They are taking his black ass to jail," my mother said between sniffles. The officer put the other woman in the backseat of a separate car. I was shocked that Pops went that route. His jump off had a swollen left eye and a couple bruises. My mom tried to beat her to death. The cops came just in time to save her. When I saw Ms. Peaches' face through the police car window, I was speechless.

I walked in the house and it was a mess. It looked like there was a struggle, and I could only imagine what really went down. I caught a glimpse of the picture of my parents' wedding day. I used to watch the wedding video and crack up. They had the wedding in Vegas and only had two witnesses, the reverend and my uncle Caleb. It looked like they were really in love when they shared their vows.

The tension between my parents had been bubbling for years. I knew that they both were in love with each other. I always wondered was that enough. I knew that had disagreements, but something like this hit me hard. I didn't want to see my father being taken away like some criminal. If I knew Camille like I thought I did, she was enjoying every minute of it. The thought alone made my blood boil.

I went down to the basement and grabbed my book bag off the back of the door. I threw some clothes and my toothbrush in it, and zipped it up. I switched sneakers and put on my rain jacket. I grabbed my keys, looked around my room, and made sure I had everything before leaving. I cut the light off and locked the door. The walk from my door to the steps felt like an eternity. I got to the bottom and hustled up the steps. My mother was yakking away to somebody on the phone. She was on the cordless and sweeping the floor.

I maneuvered around her to get to the front door. I heard my mother mumble something, but declined to get involved. I just needed to get away from the house. The rain seemed to intensify as I got closer to the bus stop. I made the walk to Spruce Street and waited under the bus stop. Lightning flashed across the sky, followed by the powerful clap of thunder. The wind picked up, sending the rain sideways. I tried to pull my hood down further to avoid it. I stepped in the street to see if I could see the lights of the septa bus. I could see it, but it was still a ways away. I wouldn't even be taking the bus if my Maxima wasn't in the shop.

I opened up my wallet and got my transpass. I pulled out my CD player and put on the radio. Soon as an R&B song came on, the 42 was pulling up to the curb. I slid my transpass through the reader and went straight to the back of the bus. There were a few people scattered throughout the bus. I turned up the volume and laid back and closed my eyes.

I had crazy days in my life, but it had nothing on tonight. I always heard stories about people's folks splitting up, but I never thought that it would be my folks. I was more worried about my brother and how he would take it. He loved seeing my parents together. That's all he knew. Me and Keon knew a one person household very well. It wasn't something I wanted Jahiem to have to deal with. I always wanted things to be comfortable for my brother. He was sheltered and never had to deal with the BS me and Keon had to go through. He deserved better.

The rain started hitting the window of the bus even harder the further we got to Center City. The office buildings and skyscrapers were coming into full view. We rode a few more blocks before I hit the yellow strip, causing the bus driver to stop the bus. I hopped off the bus and dialed Block's number.

"I need to come through."

"You aight?" Block asked with genuine concern.

"Pops got locked up not too long ago."

"You welcome to stay at the condo. Get the key from Larry. You need me, then hit me on my cell," Block said.

"Good lookin'."

"No problem. Keep your head up, my dude. I'll talk to you more about it when I see you," Block said before hanging up.

I walked around the corner and greeted the doorman before going inside the lobby. Larry was watching one of those portable TVs when I approached the desk.

"Swift, long time no see," Larry said, extending his hand. I returned the gesture. "What can I do ya for?"

"I need the key to Block's place."

"No problem. Let me get it for you." Larry went into a drawer to get the keys. After a bit of searching, he came across the key. He handed it to me and I started toward the elevator. I pushed the button and waited for it to come. When it did, a white man and women stumbled out laughing.

I got on and rode it to Block's floor. The door opened and Block's condo was right around the corner. I unlocked the door and threw my book bag on the plush beige carpet. Absolutely everything in Block's condo was neat like he was awaiting the arrival of a woman. Women loved cleanliness. Block was always on top of that.

I went straight to the bathroom. I grabbed a washcloth, toothpaste, and a bar of soap from the linen closet. I hopped in the shower for about twenty minutes and put on my basketball shorts and white T-shirt.

I was starving, so I looked through Block's freezer. I found some Steakums and some French fries. I took out the Foreman grill and a pan to put the fries on. I turned the nozzle to 350 and put the fries in the oven. I plugged the grill in and waited for it to heat up. Once it did, I threw two steaks on there. The smell was intensifying my hunger.

I went to Block's stocked bar and grabbed a Smirnoff from one of the six packs. I twisted the cap and drank it while my food cooked. I sat on the window sill and looked out the window at the lights in downtown Center City. Times like those made me think of my biological mother. *I wondered what kind of job she would have had. What would we talk about?* I looked to the sky like she could see me and smiled.

I grabbed another Smirnoff and put it on a on the coffee table on a coaster. I kicked back on the couch and flipped through the channels. Of course, it wasn't anything good on, so I turned to On-Demand and watched *The Wire*. It was Season 3 which was my favorite.

I jumped up and my food was done. I cut the oven and grill off, then made my Steakum sandwich. I covered both in ketchup and lay on the couch. It took me a whole episode to finish my meal. It was always like that when I watched *The Wire*. I had one more Smirnoff before I was in a deep sleep.

The next morning, my cell phone alarm was going off until I hit the snooze button. I got maybe five more minutes of sleep before I finally got up. I rubbed my eyes and stretched before I took my morning bathroom visit. I staggered to the bathroom. I barely had one eye open as I removed the Smirnoff from my system.

I washed my hands, brushed my teeth, and washed my face. The steaming hot water woke me up in an instant. After I got fully dressed, I poured me a cup of coffee. I put extra sugar in it just to make sure it was just right. I drank two cups before I grabbed my bag and was out the door.

When I got downstairs, I gave Larry dap before I got outside. I called my voicemail to check my messages. I had one new message from Jalen.

"Yo, Swift, I parked the Benz in Block's garage. I gave the keys to Block, too. Hit me when you get this. One."

I was glad, too, because I didn't even feel like driving it. I felt out of place in it. When I first got it, I wanted to show it off, but it didn't feel right. I never wanted to feel like I was some charity case. Granted, my car was nearing lemon status, but I earned it. It meant something to me. I guess when it came down to it, that made me feel like more of a failure.

The bus was pulling up as soon as I stepped foot near the bus stop. I got on and took the first seat in the front. The bus was packed wall to wall. The people that were standing were clearly frustrated. When I saw one of them was an elderly lady, I offered her my seat.

"Thank you, son," she said with a smile.

"You're welcome, ma'am."

"No thanks to the rest of you rat bastards," she said as she sat down. I stood for the duration of the ride.

Soon as we got near my mother's block, I got off. I walked

a couple blocks and went around the back of the house. I noticed my mother's car was there. That meant she was definitely home. I didn't want to be bothered. I was hoping that I could get in and out. The quicker the better.

I came through the back door and of course, there stood my mother.

"What is this, Swift?" my mom said, holding my shoebox open.

"Nothing."

"All this money is nothing, boy?" my mother said, holding a stack of bills.

"I had been saving up from my job and stuff."

"Boy, you must take me for boo boo the fool, huh?" my mother said, now standing.

"See, you got it all wr--" I tried to say. She didn't give me a chance to respond. She swung on me so hard I stumbled back and hit the dresser. She didn't get the desired effect because I blocked it.

"What the hell you do that for?"

"You selling drugs. It's bad enough your ignorant ass daddy sold heroin. Now you following in his footsteps?" my mother screamed.

"You don't know shit. You never were interested in my dreams, my goals, or my life. All you do is complain, whine, and bitch. I would have cheated on your ass, too." I felt the pit of my stomach burn as soon as I said that.

"Well, you can take your sorry ass money and find your own damn house since you big ballin' now. I guess you got it like that. Don't come back, either. If you do come back, the locks gon' be different." She rested her hands on her hips.

"Cool, I'll be gone in a minute," I said as I started gathering a couple more things.

It didn't hurt my mother I was leaving. It was the fact that I didn't need her help. She needed people to depend on her. It fed her ego big time. I took the rest of the money and put it in my gym bag. Then, I left the crib and made my way back to the bus stop. With all the confusion with my mother, I forgot to do one of the things I came to do.

I dialed my answering machine hoping one of those applications came through. I had three messages.

"Hello, Stephen. This is Ronald Whitaker with Rite Aid and while you interviewed very well, we regret to infor--"

I pressed the next message button.

"Hello, Stephen. This is Sally with Superfresh. We loved your interview, but what we are look--"

I pressed the next message button a little harder this time. Frustration resurfaced.

"Hey Swift. It's Cianni." Although I tried to deny it, my heart bounded firmly in my chest. "I was wondering how you were doing. I got your number from Kenny. I hope you don't mind. Anyways my number is 455-7896. Hit me up if you get a chance. Bye."

Her voice always did something to me. For some reason, I deleted the message. I could have called her a while ago, but I didn't know what the hell to say. I did the next best thing and lied to my self about the feelings I had for her.

* * * * *

Block hit my cell and told me he was downtown. I went down there and parked my car in his garage. I walked to the elevator and got off on his floor. When he opened the door, some Spanish chick bounced her thick thighs down the hallway.

"You feeling her?" Block said, leaning against the door laughing.

"Hell yeah."

"You know she got a twin sister. You say the word and I'll

hook it up for you." Block closed the door and we walked to the elevator. Once we got off the elevator, we hopped in the Jag.

"Man, where we going now?"

"You'll see when we get there," Block said with a smirk.

Déjà vu immediately set in.

"Uh oh, let me put my seatbelt on."

It was no telling what Block had up his sleeve this time.

CHAPTER 13
BLOCK

Block merged into traffic and was doing at least ninety up the highway. Drivers beeped their horns and screamed obscenities out their windows. He moved in and out of the lanes like a skilled Nascar driver. He got a rush out of driving fast. He had been doing it since he could remember. His impatience really showed on the road. He did anything to get around a slow driver. He hit their exit swiftly like finish tape awaited them. After a few miles, he finally saw the sign for Old New Castle. He made an immediate right, then left. He parked in a spacious driveway and cut the engine. The sight before them was cinematic. There were huge, gray lion heads on both sides of the brick driveway. An old school, money green Jaguar sat in the driveway. A few feet from the stairs, you could see the water. The house had four levels and was cream colored. It was one of many houses owned by Caliente.

Swift and Block walked up to the massive door, and Block pushed the doorbell. A linebacker-sized dude came to the door with an ice grill. Block matched his ice grill, inching closer to his black P89.

"And y'all are?" the linebacker said with his arms folded.

"I'm here to see Caliente," Block said. Before an argument

could ensue, Caliente's bodyguard came to the door.

BK gave Block dap, and the trio proceeded to walk into the house.

"Caliente is on the deck in the back," BK said while leading them there.

Block pulled the glass door to the right, then he and Swift stepped onto the wooden deck. The setting was peaceful and serene. The birds were chirping and the grass was precisely cut. Caliente was there, dressed in a black and white sweat suit, sipping his usual Henny and Coke. Caliente was an imposing figure. He looked like a bodyguard himself. The sweat suit he was wearing showed his muscle structure, even though it was loose fitting. His hair was graying on the sides and he wasn't ashamed. He embraced his age. He knew that those young kids couldn't tell him anything. He offered them a seat, and they both gladly accepted.

"I see your handling business out on them streets," Caliente said in between sips of his Henny and Coke.

"You know I been putting in that OT," Block said, grabbing a cigar from the holder on the table. Caliente's wife clipped the top of the cigar and lit it for Block.

"You guys are welcome to anything you like. Matter fact, Sierra, could you bring a couple drinks. Is that cool with you gentlemen?"

"Yeah," Block said, still puffing away on his Cohiba.

Sierra came back and sat down a bottle of Louis the XIII. She sat down two glasses and popped the cork off the champagne. She poured it 'til it threatened to bubble over the rim.

"So, this is the infamous Swift I've been hearing about?" Caliente said, extending his hand.

"Nice to meet you, sir, you have a magnificent home," Swift said, accepting the handshake. Caliente lit up his own cigar and began smoking.

"Hard work got me where I am. Never forget that," Caliente said, pointing his cigar. "Let's get down to business. You pay me our agreed on price and we can get the ball rolling."

The men proceeded to exchange products. Caliente checked the money, and Block checked the inventory he was given. The suitcase was packed with E pills. Caliente and Block knew in three weeks tops, it would be gone. The men drank and talked more about business. After they were done talking business, Caliente showed them the rest of his home.

Everything was custom built per Caliente's specific details. The floors had intricate patterns with white and gold trim. His initials were on the floor as soon as you set foot into the foyer. The first room that he showed them was his study, which was in the basement. The shelves in the room were filled with books. Many of which were stacked on the long, cherry wood desk. Caliente was very into obtaining information. It could be about world events or ancient history. He showed them knickknacks, shot glasses, and collectible items from several different countries. Most of them were one of kind items. Caliente loved exclusivity.

They came back upstairs and went to the garage. He hit a button on the remote, lifting the gate. When the gate was fully lifted, it revealed two matching Ferrari Roadsters. One was purple and one was black. The shine on both vehicles were professionally done. He hit the button, closing the garage door.

After he showed them around a little more, he saw them to the door.

"Oh, I almost forgot about you, Swift. Sierra, can you please get the envelope off the dining room table."

Sierra came in a few seconds later and handed Caliente the manila envelope.

"I understand you are a big basketball fan."

"Yeah. The Sixers to death."

"Good to know. Since you are now family, take this as a gift from your new family."

Swift accepted the envelope, but felt kind of awkward accepting it.

"Thank you, sir."

"No problem. You just make sure you enjoy yourself."

Block and Caliente embraced one more time before he and Swift went back outside to the car.

"What you think?"

"I'm definitely trying to live like that," Swift said, his eyes wide and full of hunger.

Block could only laugh. He knew that the lifestyle was beginning to wrap Swift up.

"What's in that envelope?"

"Man, I'm scared to find out."

Swift tore the envelope too hard and the contents fell to the ground. When he picked them up, he was speechless. They were floor seats to Sixers and Lakers. He showed them to Block, who wasn't surprised.

"That's Caliente for you."

"You told him, didn't you?"

"Naw, homie know every damn thing. He knew what school I went to before I even told him."

"That's scary, but I ain't giving these tickets back, though."

"I bet you ain't."

They both got in and Block pulled off and cut on WDAS. He turned the volume up and was instantly relaxed.

Philly's skyline was slowly approaching as they made their way across the bridge. Block hit the exit and made the fifteen-minute drive to South Philly.

"I gotta make a few stops right quick."

"Do you."

Block parked the car and hopped out like a movie star embracing the paparazzi. The dudes huddled around the entrance of the Chinese joint stared Block down until he was out of their view. Block smirked at the young boys who didn't know any better. The little kids played flag football in the middle of the street when Block turned the corner.

Block walked up to the third house from the right. The street was blocked off for a cookout. When he made eye contact with Rashad, he took off running as fast as he could. Like lightning, Block pulled his gun and cocked it back. He put a bullet into Rashad's calf, causing him to tumble into a trashcan. Everybody diverted their attention to Block.

Block walked slowly 'til he was right on top of Rashad.

"You ain't dumb enough to kill me in front of--"

His arrogant statement was cut short by the single bullet Block put into his forehead. His eyes were wide open and the sight of his exposed brain caused the women to scream. Block tapped his pockets until he came across a roll of money with a rubber band wrapped around it. He unfolded it and noticed it was a one hundred dollar bill and a bunch of ones. He kicked Rashad as hard as he could before strolling off. He came up to Swift like he didn't just commit a murder.

"We out."

He pulled out his cell phone and dialed Chante.

"What's up, baby girl?" Block said smoothly.

"Nothing, I just got out the shower," Chante said in a sensual tone.

"Me and Swift coming through later on, ma."

"What time, baby?"

"Half hour at the most," Block said, looking at his Roberto Cavalli wristwatch. "One more thing, love."

"Yes?"

"Tell Tasha to come through."

"No doubt."

"I'll see you in a few," Block said before hanging up.

The guys at the corner were no longer there, probably due

to the gunshots they heard. When Block got in, Swift was at a loss for words. Out the corner of his eye he looked over at Block in disbelief. It was the first time he had saw Block kill somebody. He saw him pull his gun, sure, but he never took it to the next level. What scared Swift the most was that his anger level never seemed to rise. He just wanted to get as far away from there as possible. Something told him it wouldn't be the last time he would hear gunshots.

M.Q.W.

CHAPTER 14
SWIFT

Block pulled into Chante's driveway and parked the car. I waited in the car while Block went to get Chante and her friend. It had been a wild day already. The more I thought about what went down earlier, I knew it was just part of the game. I pushed it out my mind and tried to focus on enjoying myself. I was looking out the window and noticed that the other girl looked real familiar. It clicked inside my head after a minute. She walked into Foot Locker the day I got fired. She was just as bad as the first time I saw her. The trio walked to the car, and she got in the backseat with me.

"How you doing? I'm Swift," I said, introducing myself.

"I'm Natasha," she said, extending her hand to me. We talked the entire trip. We covered everything in that short time span. Her body was jaw dropping and on top of that, she was articulate. I was definitely feeling her.

We drove down Delaware Ave. to Riverview. We parked around the corner and got into the ticket line. Soon as we got there, both girls wanted snacks. We went in with two tubs of popcorn and four Sprites. The movie was a lot funnier than I expected. We were all laughing right along with the crowd. I started a conversation with Natasha, temporarily ignoring the movie.

"I'm hungry, how about you?"

"A little bit. That popcorn ain't do nothing for me," Natasha said, rubbing her well-toned stomach.

"I see you ate it real quick though," I said, eyeing the empty popcorn tub.

"I mean, I ain't afraid to eat. I don't know what chicks you used to. If I see food, I'm eating it all, honey."

"That's what's up, but how do you keep it off?"

"I work out at least three times a week."

"Athletic and cute. That's a deadly combination."

"Stop making me blush, boy," she said, turning her face away from me.

Before I knew it, the credits were rolling. People were stepping over each other to get out the theater. Block and Chante got up first, and we followed them out. The girls wanted to go down Center City to shop. Their first store; Victoria's Secret.

We dropped them off and found a parking spot near the Gallery. That was rare in itself and Block never parallel parked faster. We walked up the street and went in and down the escalator. We split up and went our separate ways. After about a half an hour of shopping, we both had two hands full of bags. After I got a couple of magazines, we met up at the food court.

"You feeling Tasha, huh?" Block asked, already knowing the answer.

"Hell yeah, I could definitely see her being my main jawn."

"She is bad though. Good thing you saw her again, right."

"Man, I didn't know if I was ever gon' see her again."

"Soon as you told me what she looked like, I hit Chante. It was a coincidence that they were friends."

"That's a damn good coincidence."

We went back up the escalator and outside to the car. Block fired up the wheel and drove back over to Victoria's Secret.

We were double parked for five minutes before they walked out, holding five bags a piece. Block popped the trunk and they put the bags in.

"Y'all wanna go to Friday's since it ain't too far away?" Block said looking in the rearview.

We all nodded in agreement.

The place wasn't that packed, so we got seated right away.

"Table for how many?"

Block put up four fingers and the hostess grabbed four menus and led us to a booth.

We ordered wings and drinks, and just chilled and had a good time with each other. I hadn't had that much fun in a while, and I really needed it, too.

"I know you want that last wing, stop being shy."

I smiled and felt something stir in my chest. The way she talked, unafraid to state her opinion. The way she smiled. Even the way she smelled made me think of Cianni, and suddenly memories of my ex flooded my psyche.

Tasha tapped me in the middle of my daydreaming.

"Where you at, boy?" Tasha said, laughing.

"Yeah, Swift, you ain't hear that waiter fall and drop that food?" Block asked. "He spilled it all over that couple." Block joined in on the laughter. I looked over and saw the couple covered in food. It was funny, too. I laughed and thanked God for a least a reprieve from having thoughts of Cianni.

As we all prepared to leave, I told Block, "We'll meet y'all in the car."

He looked at me, nodded, and said, "Aight."

I focused my attention back on Tasha as Block and his girl left the restaurant.

"Look, I'm feeling you like that," I said. "I ain't with the game playing, so I was wondering if I could call you sometime."

"If you give me your phone number, I'll think about it,"
Tasha responded. I knew it was a 50-50 shot. I punched my
number into her cell phone.

"You better call me, too," I said playfully. I was dead
serious though.

* * * * *

I had to get up early for my latest job interview. I tried to
be as positive as my situation would permit. The previous
night took my mind off things for a while.

I got up and brushed my teeth, washed up, and got dressed
in my best interview clothes. I made sure I smelled fresh and
was glad my braids weren't fuzzy.

The bus ride to Center City was long and my mind was
running a mile a minute. I kept thinking of myself as a failure.
It wasn't like I was some type of slacker looking to live off
my parents forever. Everybody wanted to be a fireman, police
man, or a basketball player. All that was garbage to me. I
remember I wanted to come up with slogans for commercials.
I just knew that one of my slogans would be featured in a
Super Bowl commercial. I just wanted to do something
different than the norm. On top of filling out applications, I
was on Careerbuilder.com everyday.

The job I was interviewing for sought an applicant with
a degree in marketing. I knew I was qualified and I was
confident I could do the job. Although I may have not had
the years, I had the paper that I thought would take me over
the top.

The bus stopped at the corner and I got off and walked
to the building. I pulled out the folded paper and made sure
I had the correct address. I went through the revolving glass
door straight to the receptionist.

"Hello, do you know what floor this is on?" I said, handing

her the paper.

"Yes, sir. That office is located on the sixth floor."

"Thank you."

I walked to the elevator and I felt like I was walking in slow motion. The closer I got to the elevator, the further it seemed. When those doors slid open, I got on and watched the door shut.

I closed my eyes and whispered, "Please, let me get this job." I repeated it, each time with greater anxiety building in me.

When the doors opened, I walked out the elevator with leaden feet and rattled nerves.

If I didn't get hired, I was finished looking for a nine to five.

Chapter 15
Block

After dropping Swift and Tasha off the night before, Block chilled at Chante's house. They spent half the night cleaning and loading guns. She was almost as good as Block was. She wore blue plastic gloves while she loaded each bullet into the clips. She passed Block the purple haze. They took pulls while passing it back and forth. He blew the smoke out the window and thought about his life. He was a millionaire, but he still felt like something was missing. It was mostly his father's fault. Block recognized it only took one moment to change a life forever, and his father had surely given him that one night.

His one night started at home, with his father picking through his plate, anger resonating all throughout his face.

"Sharon, why you overcook this nasty food?" Block's father asked.

"It's not overcooked," Sharon said. "You're just drunk, goddamn it."

Block was in the living room watching a movie when his mother went into the kitchen. When he followed, he saw his mother up against the wall and his father's hand tightly around her neck. Block's father always used an excuse to beat on her.

"What you doing?" Block asked, tired of being scared.

"Talking. Now, go watch TV 'fore you be next," Block's father said in a drunken slur.

"I ain't afraid of you no more," Block shouted, flipping his old man the bird.

"You a funny little dude."

Without warning, he let go of Sharon and walked toward Block. Sharon sat on the floor holding her throat. When he got to Block, he put his fist into his chest. Block flew into the kitchen table, knocking everything on the floor.

"Get up!" his father growled.

When Block started breathing regular, he darted upstairs to his parents' room. He went right for the closet. He moved the sneakers and tore the loose floorboard off. He took his father's gun and just stared at it. Here was a man who was supposed to protect them, but instead, he did the opposite. He threw a nearby picture of his dad on the floor.

He palmed the gun and cocked it back. The gun gave Block power he'd never felt before. He felt like shooting his father until the clip was empty. He checked under his bed, and the suitcases were still there. As he got up, he heard his father's footsteps approaching.

"It's your turn now," he hollered. Block's father had blood on his knuckles and wife beater. Block feared the worst had happened. It didn't help that he didn't hear his mother's sobs anymore. He just stood there, looking at his old man. He then closed his young eyes and squeezed the trigger, twice. His father took one in the leg and shoulder. The leg shot took him down to the ground.

Finally, he was the one begging. Block loved every minute of it.

"Rick, don't do this," his father pleaded. "My job is just messing with me right know. I promise it will never happen again."

M.Q.W.

Block put the gun to his father's sweat-soaked brow. He closed his eyes and said a silent prayer.

"Ricky. No, not this way. This is the easy way for him," Sharon said, half mumbling, holding her jaw. Block threw the gun in the dirty clothes hamper and collapsed into his mother's arms.

"We have to get out of here, Mama," Block said, looking up at his mother.

"I know, baby. Grab those bags and let's go." Block took one last look at his father and left with his mother. They drove until they reached South Philly. They were far from the suburbs and that's the way they wanted it. They hadn't looked back since.

"Baby, fill this up for me," Block said, handing Chante another dutch. He watched her dump the guts, fill it, and lick it like a weed pro. She handed it back to Block after she ran the lighter through it. He blew more smoke clouds, wondering what his father was doing at that moment.

Did he really love me or my mother? Block thought. After his smoking session, he put his weed in the ashtray.

Chante put the loaded weapons in the bedroom hiding spot and rejoined Block on the bed.

"I know what will take your mind off things," Chante said, tugging at Block's Azzure sweats.

"What's that?"

Chante disrobed and stood completely nude. Soon after, her lips connected with Block's flesh, his mind completely went blank.

Block woke up early the next morning to find Chante wasn't next to him. Then, he smelled turkey bacon and cheese eggs. He damn near jumped down the entire flight of stairs chasing the aroma. When he got to the kitchen, Chante and Swift were talking.

"Good morning, y'all," Block said as he sat at the island

in the middle of the kitchen.

"Good morning," they both said, laughing even harder.

"What's so funny?" Block said, getting a little defensive.

"Look at your hand," Chante said, pointing.

Block looked down and noticed the gun in his hand. He put the safety on and put it on the table. He was smiling on the outside, but on the inside, he wished he wasn't so paranoid. He carried his gun everywhere he went. Being as rich as he was, people always wanted to get at him. He had to keep everything tight for the sake of his operation. He finished his breakfast and then got washed and dressed.

Block and Swift hopped into Block's Jaguar. Block steered the car until they were in the heart of Center City. The offices and buildings were becoming more home to Block with each passing day. He pulled into the parking garage and parked in his usual spot. He paid the parking fee, and he and Swift strolled to the elevator. They were on their way to see Block's lawyer, the one and only William "Wall Street" Brinneran.

* * * * *

After Block finished up with the meeting between him, Swift, and Wall Street, he went across town to Cadillac's spot. Block parked around the corner and made his way to the entrance. Cadillac's was a spot that Block frequented every now and then. He and Cadillac had an understanding. He saw a brother with a plan and decided to reach out. It worked out perfectly for both of them. Block provided the muscle they needed and was paid handsomely for it. It was sock drawer money for Block, but it was money nonetheless.

Cadillac's spot was set-up perfectly. In the middle of the dance floor sat a huge, rectangular bar. There were plush seats around the entire bar. Scattered throughout the surrounding area were cream colored mini couches with small tables with lamps on them. The floor was hardwood and was buffed meticulously. The lights were directly above the bar and brightened the whole area.

Nude women dancers were suspended in mid air on both sides of the huge DJ booth. The waiters were all women, wearing black and white bikini tuxedos. Their stilettos clicked hard as they sashayed through the crowd to get the patrons their drinks. Block took in the atmosphere as he approached the crowded bar. Block came to the club sometimes to let off steam or just chill. The music, mixed with the ongoing conversations, was deafening. Block tried to tune them out as he was trying to pick his poison of choice for the night.

He lifted his sleeve to get the time off his Audemars. He was going to wait for another five minutes for Caddy, then he was bouncing. The bartender came up and approached Block.

"Can I get you anything, handsome?"

"A shot of Platinum Patron."

"Coming right up."

Block scanned the dance floor to see if maybe he missed him. Soon as he turned back to the bar, Caddy was sitting in the next stool.

"Sorry I'm late. Here are the keys to the office. I had to change the locks. Oh, and the money for this month is in the safe. I gotta go, but make sure every nickel is there. If you need anything give me a call."

Block gave him a dap and hug combo and he was off just as quick as he came. The bartender came back over with his drink. She sat it on a small napkin and put two straws in it. She started wiping the already clean bar, smiling the same smile she had when Block first showed up.

Block took two gulps and put his glass back on the bar. He threw a twenty down and got up off the stool. He walked up the small staircase leading to Cadillac's office. The office smelled like Clean Linen air freshener. Block clicked the light on, walked across the cranberry colored carpet, and put the code in the safe. There were five thick stacks of money and a black Glock inside.

He sat down at the desk and put the money in the money machine that was on the desk. After the red LCD numbers told him what he wanted to know, he was satisfied. He knew cats weren't bold enough to stiff him, but he wasn't taking the chance. He closed the bag, turned off the light, and made his way back downstairs.

Soon as he came downstairs, his eyes zeroed in near the front entrance. He saw Blaze walking outside and quickened his pace. More people were coming in the club, causing him to lose Blaze in the sea of people. He wanted to bust his gun off right then and there. If he didn't have a clear shot it was useless. Soon as he got to the entrance, he saw Blaze's taillights. He was trying hard to keep his composure. Then, it hit him like a Mack truck. He pulled out his cell phone and dialed a number. When the caller picked up, he smiled.

* * * * *

Bear parked the burgundy Bentley GT in front of the Marriot near 12th and Market Street. He let Bird out and got back into the car. Bird put his gun in his waistband and zipped up his bubble coat before opening the trunk and grabbing his bag. He shifted his Kevlar vest until it was comfortable, and then entered the hotel.

"How may I help you, sir?" the voluptuous desk clerk asked with a wide grin. She was no different than any other female that lusted after Bird. She could see that he had a great build through all the layers of clothes he was wearing.

"Yeah, can I have the key for Marquis Williamson, please?" Bird asked.

M.Q.W.

After a bit of searching, the clerk handed him a key card. "Enjoy your stay."

When he got to his room, he threw his bag on the bed. He stood there for a second and enjoyed the scenery. He barely had time to chill anymore. The beef with Block took up most of his free time. He needed something good to take his mind off of it. He called up his favorite call girl, Caramel. While he waited, he grabbed some ice for the Patron he bought. He grabbed two glasses from the bar and poured the liquor in both of them. He took a few sips and waited for his entertainment to arrive.

While Bird drank, the door opened. What stood before Bird was a picture-perfect dime piece. Caramel was every man's fantasy. She had radiant skin, juicy lips, and breasts that stood at attention. She dropped her trench coat to the carpet in a swift motion. She was naked, except for an edible thong. Bird damn near dropped the glass he was holding. He admired her curves and beautiful face. Grabbing a hold of his crotch, she dropped down right in front of him and gave him $400 worth of service.

* * * * *

Blaze was pushing it by driving while intoxicated. He could barely see the road up ahead. He was really relying on instinct. Pump had warned him to stay out of the hood until things cooled off. Block's stash being taken had become national news. The streets were talking about what the retaliation would be.

Blaze was in the mood for some good food and good head. He knew he could find both within a matter of minutes. He cursed himself for drinking on an empty stomach. Luckily for him, Shelley's house wasn't that far away. He parked the car, just barely fitting inside the spot. He got in, but how he would get out was up for debate. Blaze exited the car and kept his hand near his gun. When he reached Dickinson Street, he thought he felt a presence surrounding him.

He was thinking that the liquor had him tripping. He saw a dark shadow run by and pulled his gun and cocked it back. He blinked his eyes to adjust to the nighttime. He rubbed them again, desperately trying to focus. The streetlights were doing little to help him make out the figures.

He let off a couple shots, tearing through a car mirror. When a second figure ran past, he aimed awkwardly again. That time, he trained his gun, spraying bullets back and forth. Car alarms sounded from the shattered glass. He began to sweat profusely. He wiped his forehead with the hand he was holding the gun with. It felt like he was standing in that spot and time stood still. That was the first time he feared for his life.

That's when he heard the whistle of a bullet, but couldn't pinpoint where from. The weight of the car tire collapsed on Blaze's foot. He screamed out from the excruciating pain. That sobered him up instantly. At the sight of the gunmen approaching, Blaze's eyes widened. His life began to flash before his eyes.

Trill approached Blaze, shaking his head. He then pulled out a cigarette and lit it. He took a couple puffs and smashed it into Blaze's eye socket. Blaze could only whimper as the pain shot through his entire face.

Trill finally spoke, "You a killer, huh?"

Blaze shook his head, holding his eye.

"Matter fact, no more talk for you, clown," Trill said, walking away as Stack emerged.

His screams became inaudible when the multiple bullets began spraying. Stack aimed the Calico and tore the flesh off his bones. As if nothing happened, the two men sped away in a white Escalade. Blaze lay on the curb a bloody mess and hardly recognizable.

M.Q.W.

Chapter 16
Swift

After the meeting we had downtown, I went back to my hotel. We covered a lot of things in the two hours we spent there. If something were to happen to Block, I was to take over his financial responsibilities. He trusted me enough to do that. That said a lot about our friendship. I had to get my priorities straight on my end, though. I needed to get a place to live. I definitely was done with my mother, so going home wasn't an option. I had researched houses on the internet and found some I liked. I loved the Overbrook section of the city. Block hooked me up with a well known realtor named Lori Patterson.

I planned to put every nickel I had, plus some payday loans, as a down payment. I knew it was a risk considering I didn't have a job, but I didn't care at that point. I just wanted to be in my own space and I would figure the rest out later. I was holding out hope that the job would call me back. It took every ounce of pride that I had not to pick up the phone and call back.

I hadn't spoken to my father in quite some time. I called his house line, and he answered on the second ring.

"How you doing, son?"

"Fine. I wanted your opinion on something."

"Shoot."

"I'm gon' be running with Block so I can be financially set when I start up my businesses. What do you think about that?"

"I been in this game, son, and this ain't the movies. The guns are real and so are the vultures and responsibilities that all come with it. Are you ready for that kind of pressure?"

"I know about the pitfalls of the game. I saw you in the game even when you thought I was too young to notice."

"Now, that was a different era when I was slingin', Swift. Respect was at an all-time high. These young dudes..."

There was a short pause.

"Dad."

"Son, there are decisions that you have to make on your own as a man. I can only give you my opinion. I will tell you that if you're calling for my co-sign, I can't give it to you. This isn't what I wanted for you. You have a brain inside your head, unlike most of these young dudes out here. You can use your smarts for something else."

"I hear you, Pop, but like you said, I gotta make the final decision, right? I feel like less of a man when I apply for jobs I know I'm qualified for and get the *Sorry, but* story. And, the jobs I'm *over*qualified for? Hurts worse. Nobody on the up is trying to give me a chance. I tried to do it society's way, and I'm finished."

I took a breath. Didn't realize how much anger I had until I heard the bass that laced each word.

"Well, son, it seems like you have your mind set on what you want to do. You know you get your stubbornness from your old man."

That broke the tension as we started laughing.

"Look, Swift, I love you and I'm always going to be here, no matter what your decision is."

"I love you, too, Pop. You'll see that everything will fall

into place."

"Alright, you take care of yourself, son."

"I will," I said, closing my cell.

It felt good to talk to my father. He made things seem easier. I knew it wasn't a situation where I woke up and it was my decision. That get an education speech was BS. I had been hearing it so long I started to feed into it. My choice was set in stone and talking to my father calmed my nerves for the time being.

I put the phone on the nightstand and stretched out my legs. The king size bed was ultra comfortable. I turned on the TV, hoping something half decent was on. I looked at the laminated channel guide and scanned it for HBO. When I flicked to the channel, a re-run of the *Sopranos* was on. I was half satisfied, so I watched it.

About midway through, my stomach started growling loudly. I ignored the sounds the first couple of times, then gave in. I decided to order some room service. I looked through the menu at least twice before I chose some breakfast.

I started turning channels on cable again while waiting for the food to arrive. On a commercial break, the food came, and I tore it up and fell asleep with the TV on.

* * * * *

The next afternoon, I left my hotel room, got the car from the valet, threw him a tip, and sped off. While I was on the expressway, I called Lori. We agreed to meet at her office in Center City.

Lori's secretary eyed me suspiciously before speaking. "Mr. Jackson?"

"Yes, ma'am."

"Lori's waiting for you," she said, giving me a warm smile. I walked into Lori's office and was greeted with a firm handshake. She was definitely about her business. Her office was laid out. Her desk was in the middle of the room in front of a huge window. The plants and family pictures gave it a homey feel. There were two large bookshelves on both sides of the room that spanned the whole wall.

"How are you doing today, Stephen?" Lori said, flashing a bright smile.

"I can't complain," I said, getting comfortable in the leather chair.

"I wrote down your house requirements, and I think I've found you the perfect home." She held up an 8x10 picture of the house. I loved it and told her I was ready to see it.

We pulled into a long, circular driveway in front of a three-car garage. I had only seen the outside of the house and was hooked on it. The paint was different from the photo. We both got out and took in the sight before Lori spoke.

"Well, Stephen, as you can see, this is the magnificent house I spoke about," she said with a wave of her arm. When I walked into the crib, my eyes damn near popped out my head. My mom's crib was dope, but that place was way better. The spiral staircase was marble and led up two flights.

The master bedroom was bigger than my, Malik's, and Jahiem's rooms combined. The walk-in closet was big enough to jump up and not hit your head on the ceiling. I knew because I tried it. It had four bedrooms and two and a half bathrooms. The backyard was huge and surrounded by a tall metal gate. It looked how I envisioned it would. It had a deck, swimming pool, and Jacuzzi. The basketball court just made it that much better.

Lori finished selling me on the house, though she didn't really have to. We agreed that I would be at closing by the end of the week. She told me about the minor work the house needed done. I was happy that I was going to be living on my own terms and conditions. I jetted to my mom's house to get the rest of my stuff and didn't care if it sat in my trunk. Just as long as it was gone from her house. I turned the radio to Power 99 FM en route to my mother's house. They were playing *Dirt off Your Shoulder* by Jay-Z. I had my bass vibrating the car it was so loud.

I was surprised my mom didn't change the locks. I went and sat on the living room sofa. I picked up the various pictures that lined the coffee table, and for awhile, I just stared at them, silently letting my mind drift. I finally went to my room and started ransacking it. I found things that I wasn't even looking for. I took the rest of my clothes and sneaks. I threw it all in two big trash bags.

I made my way back up the stairs before I heard a familiar sound. Jahiem skipped the steps before hitting the bottom step with both feet. He looked bigger and more mature than the last time I saw him. His little beard had become bigger. I knew what he was going to ask me before he spoke. I guess it was the look in his young eyes. The eyes were always a dead giveaway.

"What up, Swift?"

"Chillin', baby boy."

"So, you leaving like Dad did?"

"It's just time for me to go. You know how Mom can be."

"Yeah, I know, I just hope she don't try to kick me out, too," Jahiem said, laughing. I joined in with my brother, and we chopped it up a little bit. I took him to the King of Prussia Mall and let him get whatever he wanted. He let me know how appreciative he was every five minutes. I smiled. I had wanted to take my brother's mind off our parents' problems—if only for a while. I felt I had succeeded.

* * * * *

I dropped Jahiem off and before I could get out the door, my mother yelled my name. I was about to keep walking like I didn't hear her, but I went to see what she wanted.

"Your father sent you something," she said, and then continued her conversation.

"Where is it?" I said, instantly annoyed.

She gave me that over there gesture with a flick of the wrist. I went and searched the dining room table and found the letter addressed to me. I tore it open and a small card fell out. It had a phone number next to the words *Call XL*.

I left without saying another word to my mother.

In the car, I dialed the number on the card.

"Swift?"

"Yeah."

"Meet me at the corner of 23rd and Ellsworth."

"Aight."

"One."

I pulled up and parked on Alter Street. I got out and walked to the corner where an old bar used to be. After a few minutes of waiting, a white limo pulled up and abruptly stopped.

The driver side door swung open, and a guy got out and opened the back door for me. He looked salty for some reason. I got in the back seat, and it felt like a living room. The man who I was assuming was XL got off his cell phone as soon as I sat down. He had on a gray pin-striped suit that hugged his large frame.

"Nice to finally meet you," he said, extending his hand.

"Same here."

"I know you're confused as to why we're meeting today."

"A little."

"I used to be your Pops' right hand man. When we stopped hustling, we kind of lost touch. He's the one who gave me my nickname XL. A year ago, we hooked back up, and he helped me get back on my feet. Your Pops said that he thought I

M.Q.W.

could help you now."

"Definitely, I think we can do something. What I'ma do is talk to my man and make sure everything is straight. Make sure you stay in touch though."

"No doubt, and don't worry about Ceaser," XL said, nodding to the dude who held the door open, "he don't like nobody. "

We shared a laugh.

Back at 23rd and Ellsworth, Ceaser stopped the car. I gave XL dap and exited the car. As I walked down the sidewalk, I shook my head. Pops was always a step ahead of me, and if he was getting me hook ups now, I couldn't help but wonder what the game had in store for me.

CHAPTER 17
BLOCK

After his failed attempts, Block didn't want Swift to be involved in the nasty underworld he dealt with on the regular basis. He wanted him just to get money, but realized that the ugly part was a package deal. He saw plenty that justified his reasons. Swift didn't know it, but it made Block furious that he wasn't receiving any call backs from those jobs. He knew that Swift's whole thing was to stand on his own two feet. If more dudes stood on their own, it would be fewer problems. Those grimey dudes just weren't built like that.

Block sat down on the couch and leaned his head back. The day had taken a lot of energy out of him and he needed rest. He leaned forward and poured him a shot of vodka. He took it to the head, welcoming the burn. The sky was slowly changing colors and Block was just about to take a short nap before his intercom buzzed. Block got up and walked over and pressed the button.

"Yo, who that?"

"It's me."

Block immediately pressed the button, allowing Swift to enter. He could hear the difference in Swift's voice and became concerned. A few minutes later, Swift came through the door looking like he wanted to kill something or someone. Block offered him a seat and a drink. He accepted both. Block poured him a drink, handed it to him, and prepared to listen.

"I mean, I did everything right and them crab ass dudes still ain't call me back," Swift said, downing the shot of vodka.

Block poured him another one. He took that one to the head before he spoke again.

"What the hell am I supposed to do now?" Swift said, sounding defeated.

"Whatever you need, baby boy, I got you."

"That offer still stand?"

"Look, I th—"

"Naw, Rick, I'm cool with it."

Once Block heard Swift use his government, he knew that it was a problem. He hadn't called him Rick in a long time. Block didn't want to put his best friend in any danger, but Swift had made up his mind, so he rolled with it.

Swift got pretty hammered during the course of his and Block's conversation. Block wasn't letting him drive alone, so he drove him home himself. First, Block ran a couple errands and when he came back Swift was still sleep. He was slobbering and snoring. He woke Swift up and helped him to the car. He opened the passenger door and guided him to the seat. He closed the door and hopped in the driver's seat. He fired up the car and navigated through Center City until he was in Overbrook.

The way Block drove, it didn't take long for them to get to Swift's house. He got an incoherent Swift out the car; he shook his head and laughed.

He got Swift up stairs successfully and unlocked his door. Block helped Swift on the couch and removed his Timberland boots. He walked to the closet and got a blanket to cover him with. After he made sure Swift was still breathing, he left. He checked the door one more time and hopped back in the car.

Before he pulled off, he couldn't stop thinking was he making the right decision in regards to Swift. Maybe if Swift had the chance to sleep on it he would change his mind. Block pulled off and knew that's exactly how it would play out. He was sure of it.

* * * * *

Block awoke to a message from Swift cementing the fact that he was ready to make money. Block sat on the edge of his bed shaking his head. There was only one thing to do. He had to make sure that his partner had every advantage he could give him. It was a dirty game and those dudes definitely never played fair. Right after his gun inspection, he went into his huge bathroom and got prepared for his day, which was full of activity. After he was clean, he put on the oil he copped from 52nd Street. Then, he used an afro pic on his sunni. When he was satisfied with his appearance, he went into his walk in closet. His closet went back at least twenty yards.

He tore open a fresh pack of wifebeaters, pulled one out, and put it over his head. He looked to his immediate left and grabbed the double breasted bulletproof vest and strapped it on. He chose the quickest outfit he could, which was what he did on days like that. Any other time he might have opted for a suit, but today was a chill day. He grabbed a stack of black long sleeves, grabbed one, and tossed the rest to the ground. He chose a pair of Diesel jeans and a pair of black Timberland field boots. To make his ensemble complete, he grabbed the gun off his nightstand and put it on his waist. He was fresh as possible and ready to roll.

He looked out the window and Swift was pulling up. He grabbed his hoodie off the arm of the couch, put on his shades, and walked out the door. He greeted Swift with dap and a hug before getting in the passenger seat. Block gave

Swift the directions and they were in the parking lot of the gun range within a half hour. They both hopped out of the car and strolled to the entrance.

"Ain't no turning back," Block said as he held the door open.

Swift nodded and said, "Let's do this."

* * * * *

After he had spent nearly half the day with Swift, Block decided to visit his mother's Villanova home. It had been a minute since he had last seen her. When Block pulled up to the front, her car was parked in the driveway. When he opened the door to his mom's crib, it smelled like Vanilla Lace candles. The scene looked choreographed for something freaky. The radio hummed slow music throughout the house. Block couldn't help but think that he walked into a prepared date. He got confirmation when his mother swung around the corner in her bra and panties.

"Hey ba--," Sharon said before covering herself up and stuttering. She quickly ran in her bedroom and slammed the door behind her. "Boy, what you doing here?" she said behind the closed door.

"I was in the neighborhood and decided to stop by," Block said, laughing at his mother.

Block's mother came out her room with sweatpants and a white T-shirt. She turned the oven off, blew out the candles, and turned off the radio.

"You thought I was Nick?"

"Yeah, he said he was coming by at 4:30," Sharon said.

In the middle of their conversation, her cell phone went off. It seemed like soon as she got on it, she got off it.

"He said he can't make it."

"That's cool, I'll take you somewhere. How about that?"

"I would love that. At least somebody cares about me."

Block and his mother embraced each other. At that moment, Block felt like a little boy again. He was a stone cold gangster, but always felt safe in his mother's little arms.

"You ready, Ma?"

"Give me like fifteen minutes." He knew that meant an hour in woman speak. He cut on the cable and watched ESPN for a little while. His mom came strolling downstairs forty-five minutes later. They left the house and got in Block's truck.

His mother was hungry, so they went through McDonald's drive-through. As he drove, Block could have sworn somebody was following them. He just chalked it up to being a little paranoid. He shook it off and kept on driving. When they reached Center City, Block drove straight to his garage and parked the vehicle.

"Boy, what do you have planned this time?"

"We gon' go cop a few things. I know how much you love jewelry. Plus, you always say how you wanna shop on Fifth Avenue."

"We should have taken your car up there then, boy."

"I can't take a break once and awhile?"

"This ain't about no break. You gettin' that damn car today, ain't you?"

She knew what he was thinking before his mouth even said it. That playboy smile confirmed her suspicions.

From there, they walked the city streets until they reached the Greyhound bus station. It gave them a chance to talk to each other, which they rarely did anymore. They purchased their tickets and waited outside for the bus.

Within a couple minutes, the bus pulled up, and they both boarded it. The ride took a little longer due to traffic. At one point, Block's mother fell asleep. Block just typed away on his laptop. He was calculating the figures on the waterfront condominiums in Delaware. They were set to be completed by the middle of 2005.

The bus driver pulled them into New York straight through the Lincoln Tunnel.

He knew his mother would appreciate the gesture. Between her new boyfriend and his status, there wasn't time for them to do anything with each other. The traffic finally died down as they pulled into the bus station in Manhattan.

Soon as they got off the bus, Block flagged a cab down.

When the cab pulled up he helped his mother in the back seat like she was elderly.

"Boy, I ain't that old, yet."

"Where to, my friend?" the cab driver said in a heavy accent.

"Fifth Avenue."

They pulled up to the array of stores that lined Fifth Avenue. Block gave his mother his black card and told her to call his cell if she had any problems. He gave her a kiss on the cheek and left. He instructed the driver to drive him to the car dealership.

At the dealership, he spotted L right away. L was no doubt kicking game to the couple before him. Block watched the couple shake L's hand and hop into a brand new truck. When L finished his sale, Block approached him.

"What up, L?" Block said, extending his hand.

"I just got the Maybach yesterday, I know that's what you came for," L said, smirking and twirling the keys. "You gon' kill Philly wit' this. I know for a fact you the first to cop this. Be ready for the unwanted attention. You think you were being envied before? You ain't seen nothing yet."

"In these streets, I'm untouchable," Block said. "Philly ain't neva seen a better hustler. They never will either."

"I know all too well."

"How much I owe you?"

"450."

"Dollars?" Block said sarcastically before pulling out a street curb thick stack of bills. He then handed a bag to L, taking the keys in return.

"I'll handle the technicalities for you as usual," L said. "I'll call you when everything is situated."

"Thanks again, L."

"No problem, Block. Make sure you keep your eyes open and watch your back."

"Aight, L, I catch you next car purchase," Block said, walking to the black-on-black Maybach Benz. He was wondering what his mom was doing, so he called her.

"Hey, baby, did you get your car?"

"Yeah, I'm driving it now. Where you at?"

"At the spa getting my feet and nails done."

"Cool, I'll be back Monday to take you home. I'm goin' to head back to Philly to take care of some business. I think you need a little weekend vacation anyway."

"Okay, baby. Before you go, what's the limit on this credit card?"

"Unlimited."

"Alright then, let me get off this phone and spend," Sharon said, laughing as they ended their conversation.

It didn't take long for Philly's skyline to appear. He pulled up to the parking garage and parked his new toy. He briskly walked to his building with his hand on his gun. It was the second time he had that crazy feeling. For the second time that day, he brushed it off.

CHAPTER 18
SWIFT

I had every single thing out of my mother's house, finally. The truth was that I wasn't immediately ready to bounce. My mother pushed me to my limit. A man could only turn the cheek so many times before he felt like it was being slapped. I could remember distinctly the argument me and my mother had over me going to school and potentially moving out.

I was coming home from one of those job hunting days. It was a heat wave warning and I still had my suit on. I just really wanted to look the part. Professionalism was very important to me. I stepped inside the house and draped my suit jacket over the dining room chair. The central air was much appreciated. I could hear footsteps coming and knew it was my mother. She walked right by me without even acknowledging my presence. It wasn't like I was surprised, but it didn't stop it from being disrespectful though.

I never did anything to remotely disrespect my mother. I would admit that I wasn't feeling the situation at first. I felt like she was trying to replace my mother. Nobody could fill her shoes as far as I was concerned. I was tired of beating around the bush, so I just came out and said what was on my chest.

"Did you look over the information that I emailed you?"

"Yeah."

I was waiting for some type of elaboration. After she wouldn't volunteer one, I went ahead.

"So, do you think that it can be done? Because I can't get financial aid because y'all make too much money."

She let out one of those sarcastic laughs and knew I was instantly pissed off. I knew my cheeks were red then. Every time I was upset, it happened.

"Swift, I want to be upfront as possible. It is my decision not to waste money on somebody who was a below average high school student. I don't even know if you would even finish school. You came within an inch of getting kicked out, remember?"

I did remember, but I had stored it away as the past. It was something that I overcame and graduated. That didn't matter to my mother. She was the absolute best at finding a negative in a pile of positive.

"Of course I remember. But, what does that have to do with this situation?"

"It has everything to do with it. You want to move on your own, too. Do you know how much it costs to maintain a household?"

She was firing off questions trying to get me to break. I was too hip to her by now.

"Of course I researched everything. I've never jumped into anything without doing my homework first."

"Look, son, I'm just not confident about this. I think you need to give these things some thought first, and then make a decision about school and moving."

She tried to play that concerned parent bit. I wasn't buying it.

"You're right, I should give it some thought."

Yeah right.

I had the people redo the house design. All the loose wiring was corrected. The Jacuzzi and swimming pool were cleaned thoroughly. I had the lawn manicured and the house repainted. It was taking shape slowly but surely.

I spent most of my time in my office. I kept all my records stored there. I had electronic strips installed in the doorway to the office, so if the computer was taken past that point the hard drive was completely wiped clean. It wasn't like in a CSI episode; there would be no recovering the files.

I kept the count of every corner we had. I made sure that every captain had the receipts for the day's earnings. I had a safe built into the floor in the basement for record keeping. I kept a certain amount of money there as well for emergency purposes. I kept a .45 in my drawer even though I wasn't worried about nobody doing anything.

Block ran his business with an iron fist. I remember one time I went to collect the receipts from one of the corners in North Philly and ran into a little problem. I was a little nervous, seeing as though I was a new jack. Stack rolled with me just in case something jumped off. He pulled up in a silver Durango, bumping Philly's Most Wanted's *Please Don't Mind*.

He hit the button, unlocking the door. I hopped in the truck and closed the door. He opened the glove compartment and got a gun, leather gloves, and a silencer. He put the gloves on and screwed the silencer on the barrel. He moved as if he were brushing his teeth – just an everyday ritual. Soon as he sat the gun on his lap, he gave me a fist-pound.

We rode in silence until we came up to corner, cut the lights, and parked.

"That's homie right there," Stack said, pointing to the middle of the block.

We both hopped out and went opposite directions. I walked up to Trey, who was clowning with his boys. Soon as I got close enough, they all jumped, which told me they weren't on point.

"What you need, pimp?" Trey said before spitting on the sidewalk.

"Naw, family, I'm here to collect," I said.

"The problem is, I don't know you. And, neither do my people. You police, homie?"

Soon as the last words left his tongue, they all pulled out on me. I stood there because they couldn't see Stack dressed in all black. He seemed to blend in with the dark surroundings.

He fired a shot, which sounded like a bird's chirp. It dropped Trey to his knees, causing him to drop his gun. Once Trey fell, his boys turned to see the gunman clutching a pistol. They froze, knowing they were screwed.

"Yo, Stack, we wa--"

He put the gun to his lips, signaling silence. He shot both of them once in the foot, leaving them hopping around like two idiots.

"I catch y'all out here again, I ain't aiming below the waist," Stack said. "Dig me?"

They all nodded, scooting back to the brick wall. I just stared at them as they looked on in fear. From that point on, whenever I went to collect, I got the same respect as if Block was coming to get the receipts himself.

* * * * *

After I collected every nickel that was owed, I took the money to Block's grandmother's house on 49th and Walnut. I gave Ms. Lillian a hug and a kiss before I went downstairs. I divided the money up in two halves of $50,000. I put one half in the basement wall and took the rest with me. I left out the back of the house and shot over to Block's condo. I gave Larry a fist-pound and kept it moving. I took the elevator up and gave Block dap as he opened the door.

"How we doing this week?"

"Even better than last week," I said, tossing Block two bags. One was full of money and the other was full of receipts.

Later that evening, we all went to Cadillac's nightspot. We walked in the building and commanded everybody's attention. I went to place some bets downstairs in the basement. I put some paper on the Eagles and Sixers. I went buck wild and blew easily a couple thousand down there on them tables.

Had that been a couple months ago, I would have been tripping. There would be no money to blow on the tables. There would be no fast cars and even faster money. Now that I had it, every once in a while, I thought, *why not?* After playing the rules like a good boy – going to college, working straight-laced jobs, then getting kicked down one too many times, I thought it was truly my time to shine now, so I did. I flossed it up, while all my damn degree did was take up wall space.

The new me partied and enjoyed myself. I couldn't even begin to tell you how good it felt to own my own things.

I eventually went back upstairs to the dance floor. There were women everywhere. A vanilla wafer skinned chick started grinding on me. I tried my best to match her moving hips. I wasn't the best dancer, but I was doing my two-step thing. How she managed to fit all that into those jeans was a mystery. She grinded everything she had to Usher's *Yeah*.

After the song ended, I went over to VIP section. My peoples were crowding the reserved space. Trill, Stack, and Block were playing pool and talking trash.

"Bet then," Block said, throwing a stack of money on the white pool table.

"Triple that," Trill said, throwing two rubber banded stacks on the table. Block had already beaten Stack. His pool game was tight, but ya boy was a pro. After he finally disposed of Trill, I stepped up.

"I bet you $5,000."

"Naw, baby, put some more paper up," Block said. "I already won seven grand. I'm unstoppable."

"Your loss then," I said, pulling $10,000 out of my back pockets. I threw it on the table next to Block's $7,000.

"Break," Block said, clutching the pool stick by his side. I didn't give Block one shot on the table. I took the $17,000 without breaking a sweat.

After we shook the groupies, we took the fleet of cars to the South Street Diner. I was a little hungry, and by the way everybody was ordering, I knew they were, too. When the food came, it looked like a buffet table. We ate the grub and bussed it up with each other.

"Remember when we stole that broke down squatter that summer?" Block asked.

"Yeah, man, we got sent to juvie. I was scared of what my parents were going to do to me. Forget the fact that we were locked up," I said.

"We were some bad little kids back in the day," Trill said.

"Bad don't describe what we were," Block said.

Those were the best of times for me. I trusted all those men with my life. They treated me like their little brother.

We paid the bill and went our separate ways. I walked down near Penn's Landing where my car was, got in, and put my gun in the stash spot. I made it to my house in no time, pushing ninety. I parked in the garage, grabbed my gun, and went through my side entrance.

I checked my answering machine and had two messages from my mother and father. My mom was frantic about the people Malik was bringing through the house. Another headache nearly developed after listening to the message. My father wanted to know how my decision was going. So, I had to get back to both of them.

I went downstairs to my office and cut on the light. I

opened up the bag and emptied the stacks of money on the desk. I sat there and put every single dollar bill I collected through the money machine. While the money machine clicked, I made sure the receipts matched with my estimates. I compared both totals and was satisfied that nobody tried to short the count. I stapled all the receipts and put them along with the money in the floor safe. I took the .45 off my waist and ejected the clip. I put it in my desk drawer and went back upstairs. I went to the third floor and collapsed on my King sized bed. It didn't take long at all to fall asleep.

Chapter 19
Block

Block threw his keys on the onyx and gold coffee table and sunk into his imported leather couch. He checked some of his emails and browsed the internet. After he wrote down a couple numbers, he took a shower. He hadn't counted his house stash in a while. He pulled up a chair and plugged in the machines before taking two briefcases from the back of the fridge and cracking them open. He had done that so many times before. It still gave him a rush to see the bills stacked after being automatically counted.

After the clicks concluded, there was five million dollars between the two briefcases. A lot of people talked money, but Block was the definition of it. He made sure his money was in more than one place.

He put the stacks of money back into the briefcases and locked them. He put them in the back of the fridge and screwed it shut. Before he could put one more thing in order, Block fell asleep on the couch.

The next morning, he was up eating Cap'n Crunch and watching the news. He looked at his Vacheron wristwatch, making sure he was on time. After finishing breakfast, he got ready to run some errands. He and Swift were supposed to go to the King of Prussia Mall.

After he picked up Swift, Block drove to a corner store. Swift waited in the car while Block went in.

"What up, my dude?" Block said, greeting the gentleman behind the glass.

"Chillin', how's life treating you?" Eddie said, buzzing Block in the door.

"Great."

"The cases are down there in the back waiting for you."

Block walked behind the refrigerators and down a flight of creaky, wooden stairs. The old heads from the block had a card game going. Cigar smoke hovered above the drink glasses that were on the table. All the men acknowledged the capo when he came through. He acknowledged them back with a head nod. He got the case of forty eight sodas and took them back to the car.

Block had the majority of the Philly corners. The corner money didn't compare to the other crowd of users, the everyday stiffs that used drugs to take them away from reality. You couldn't guess how many school teachers, deacons, and doctors did heavy drugs. A lot of Block's paper came from the upper class individuals that populated cities.

Block and Swift eventually used Keon's connection with the vending machines. They could stash the E pills in the machines, and have them delivered with less hassle.

Block doubled parked in front of Popeye's and put his hazard lights on. They ordered their food and waited for the girl to come back with their orders.

"Shorty slow as hell. I know she know who I am. I come in here every other day."

All Swift could do was shake his head. He thought he was impatient, but Block couldn't stand to wait for anything. He forcefully grabbed the bags, and he and Swift strolled out the door.

Back at the car, Block said, "I'm supposed to be getting it

in with the twins tonight." He unlocked the car door.

"Hook me up, then," Swift said, laughing.

Rapid gunfire shattered the storefront window next to Popeye's. The driver's side of the Maybach was next to be showered with a hail of bullets. Swift and Block ducked inside the car. Block grabbed the .45 off his waist and the one from under his driver's seat.

Block jumped out the Maybach and shot at the gray car, putting several holes in the exterior. He erased the back window and brake lights, and flattened the left back tire. He shot until his guns clicked empty. The Oldsmobile zoomed away until it was a blur, barely escaping.

Swift got out the car and stood next to Block, who was putting the guns in his waist.

"You good?"

"Yeah," Swift said a little more calm than he really felt.

Block looked at Swift and shook his head. He put his best friend's life in danger. He knew he didn't do it purposely, but he still would have felt responsible if something happened. He turned around and looked in the direction of the car as if it was still there. The only question in Block's mind was who the hell had the balls to shoot at the King of Philly.

Swift was deep in thought as he stood there. Although he wasn't a stranger to the lifestyle anymore, that didn't change the experience. Today let him know that he was really in "the game."

* * * * *

Block's mind was still on the shootout that had occurred not even an hour ago. He had been in too many wars. The thing was that he never had family with him. He had to keep his eyes open even wider now. It wouldn't take long before he knew who was responsible. He could see, smell, and taste the blood.

Block got back downtown in record time. He parallel parked on the street and made his way into his building. He gave dap to Larry and got on the elevator. He walked in the condo and went straight to the bathroom. He didn't even want to go to the party. He wouldn't have gone, either, if it wasn't for a potential money deal down the road.

After he showered, he sprayed on Jean Paul Gaultier and made sure his waves were flowing. His clothes were laid out on the ironing board. He slipped on the crisp white dress shirt followed by a suit by Valentino. He sat on the bed and put on his dress socks and slipped on his black Louis Vuitton loafers.

He grabbed his gun and checked the clip. It was full and he tucked in his waist. He cut off the lights and was out his condo and on the elevator in no time. He rode the elevator alone and made his way outside to his car. He loved the sound of the Maybach coming to life. He pulled off toward the hotel. When he stopped in front of the hotel, the valet hurried to Block's door. He tipped him $50 and walked into the hotel.

After he got directions from the hotel clerk, he walked to the grand ballroom. There was a woman behind a podium when he got there.

"How may I help you?" she asked, giving him a warm smile.

"I'm here for the party," Block said, taking in his surroundings.

"And your name, sir?"

"Rickey Johnson."

She scanned the list and came to Block's government name nearing the end of the page. She checked him off and gave him a laminate to wear.

The doorman man opened the door and Block walked in the party with his authentic Philly bop. The chandelier in the middle of the ceiling was huge and sparkled in the midst of the bright lights in the room. The white curtains went all the way around. The crowd was very upscale. Almost every woman was covered in diamonds and wore expensive weaves. The cigar smoke was free to drift into the air. The makeshift bar was lively with activity. There were too many attractive women for him to choose just one. He never really had a girlfriend, per se. He had women, but he never became emotionally attached. He never wanted his enemies to go after somebody he cared deeply about. He pretended to be distant at all costs.

He walked through a sea of people to get to the bar. He took a seat and waited for the bartender to wait on him. After a few moments, he wiped the bar clean and walked over to Block.

"What can I do ya for?" he asked, still cleaning the bar.

"I'll have a rum and Coke. Actually, let me have two."

"Coming right up."

The waiter walked off, giving Block a second chance to scope the scene. He recognized several bigwigs scattered throughout the party. The DJ threw on Luther Vandross and the pace of the dancing changed drastically. Block was never much of a dancer. He had the two step in his arsenal but rarely used it. He preferred the woman do all the work.

The bartender bought the drinks and sat them in front of Block. He quickly threw both of them back. He looked at his Audemars and noticed he'd only been at the party for a half an hour. He was already bored. The minute he thought about leaving, money walked over.

"Mr. Johnson, I'm glad you could make it tonight."

"My pleasure, sir," Block said, shaking Matthew Strayhan's hand.

Strayhan was the biggest real estate guru on the east coast. He had put Block on to several profitable projects. He had told Block he was working on some huge deals that he should be a part of. Block knew that if he wanted to be on top of his game he had to learn from the absolute best.

After Block wrapped up his conversation and spoke with a couple more important people, he called it a night. Before he did leave, he had a couple more rum and Cokes.

He walked back through the crowd to the lobby of the hotel. The valet went to get Block's car while Block sat on one of the cranberry colored couches. The valet came through the automatic double doors and handed Block the keys. He took them and strolled back outside to the Maybach. He started the car and didn't know exactly where he was going.

He pulled out and made a right at the green light. He was in the mood for sex and went straight to Tianna's house. He could show up and just get it crackin'. Soon as he was done, he would leave for New York afterwards to pick up his mother. Block cruised the South Philly streets in the early hours of the morning. The sky was light orange and the breeze zipped through the cracked window. It was only him and one other car on the streets. Block looked in the mirror and through that the car was entirely too close for his liking. He took the gun off his waist and sat it on the passenger seat.

He made a turn to see if the driver would follow. When he got to the corner, he saw them again in his rearview. He mashed the gas and was ready for the challenge. Nobody knew the streets better than him. The car was gaining on him. When he hit a straight away, he just knew he could outrun the car. The pedal was on the floor and the objects outside were a blur. No matter how fast he went, the car was still on him. Now, it was only inches from his bumper. When the car bumped his car, he swung to the right, slamming into a parked car.

The airbag exploded into his chest and pushed him back in his seat. When he opened his eyes, he saw blood on his forehead in the rearview mirror. He had a few cuts and bruises, but was alright. He grabbed the gun off the passenger seat and opened the door slowly. The shattered glass rained on the ground soon as he did. He put the gun to his side and crept along the car listening for movement.

The unknown driver popped up, and they got into a wrestling match over the gun. Several shots fired in the midst of the struggle. He managed to get Block to drop the gun.

Once Block got leverage, he landed a jab that broke his jaw instantly. The cracking sound was sickening. When the guy was on the ground, Block tried to stomp through him with his Louis loafers. When the officers saw their own being beat severely, they rushed Block. They tackled him over the hood of the unmarked cop car. Even though he was outnumbered, he still landed a few punches that did some damage. They finally subdued him and got him into the back of the car.

Getting Block in custody was one thing, but keeping him in custody was another thing altogether.

CHAPTER 20
SWIFT

I was with Natasha at my crib when that phone vibrated. I looked over at the phone in disbelief. Natasha caught my facial expression and already knew what it was. I grabbed the phone, took the sim card out, and flushed it down the toilet. I hopped up, took a bird bath, and got dressed. I grabbed the Glock from under my bed and put the clip in. Natasha still had the covers up to her neck, remaining quiet as I moved around the bedroom like a lunatic.

"We gotta go."

She got up and started putting her clothes back on. For the moment, I looked at her naked body. Natasha was a good girl and I knew the first time I met her. She had all the qualities that I was looking for in a woman. She finally pulled up her jeans, which barely fit over her hips. She had to jump up to get them all the way up.

She packed everything she bought to my crib in her overnight bag. I sat on the bed and adjusted the gun in my waist. I opened the nightstand and grabbed some money.

She gave me a look I would never forget. She didn't have to speak. We both knew what had to be done. We made our way out the house to the truck outside. I hit the button on my key ring and the doors unlocked.

Soon as I started the car, Keyshia Cole's *Love* blared from the speakers. I wondered how the hell that was playing and then remembered that she was the last person in the truck. The thought of that made me smile.

The ride was mostly in silence except for an occasional cough from her. She looked out the window at all the cars on the highway. What the hell was I supposed to say? My mind was blank and I couldn't even start up a conversation, so I let the radio lead.

I made the same ride a hundred times, but that day it seemed like it was taking forever. I parked in front of the post office near the 30th Street station.

I got her bag out the backseat and carried it over to the train station. I directed her over to the first bench we came across.

"Listen, I kn—"

"You don't have to say anything, Swift. I knew what it was when we got together. I just want you to know that I love you. And, I'm not lame enough to demand you say it back. I just wanted you to know that, though."

All I could do was embrace her and kiss on her moist lips. Her Dior perfume seemed to whirl around me. When we broke the kiss, I made sure to get a mental picture of her. She must have read my mind because she turned around so I could get a full view. She spun back around with a smile on her face.

I busted out laughing at her silliness. I gave her one more kiss and hug before I gave her the envelope of money. I watched her strut off with her bag slung over her shoulder. Her heels clicked with every step she took. I watched her until the sound faded and she was out of view down the escalator.

I got back in the car and just sat there for a minute, taking everything in. I really had to do my thing with Block off the streets. I couldn't speak to Block until I went down to see him. On the inside, the inmates knew who he was, so I was never worried about somebody stepping out of line or anything. I just didn't want anything to fall by the way side. I didn't bother turning the CD player on because I needed complete silence.

By the time I reached my crib, all I wanted to do was sleep. Maybe when I woke up Natasha would be next to me and Block wouldn't be in custody.

* * * * *

Block got arrested on Friday and by Monday, I was at Block's condo running through it like a tornado. Anything that looked like it could potentially hurt Block, I grabbed it. I took the money he kept in the fridge. All the guns that were littered throughout the condo were all scooped up, too. I sat there with plastic gloves and cleaned each of the ten guns that were sitting on the white bath towel. When the police came there, they wouldn't get anything concrete. The last thing I did was load all the laptop's info onto memory sticks. I took one last look and went to my next destination.

I drove to the bridge and threw the guns into the Schuylkill River. Afterwards, I drove to Block's secret estate. Only Ms. Sharon and I knew about its existence. His neighborhood was low key and filled with trees. Luxury cars lined the driveways, and kids played in the street carefree. Ever since Block got knocked, I had been paranoid. I wasn't carrying my gun or that much money. I even changed clothes twice before I came.

I parked around the back of the house. I walked around to the front and unlocked the door with the spare key. The place was laid out just as I remembered. Block had every famous hustler or gangster lining the walls. Everybody from Freeway Ricky Ross to Rich and Alpo was there. The living room had everything a bachelor needed. The white and burgundy pool table sat off in the corner. The bar had seats and was stocked full of expensive liquors. I expected nothing less from Block.

I walked up a flight of stairs, searching for Block's master bedroom. I assumed it was the biggest room at first. When I saw that all the rooms were almost equal in size, I was stumped. The picture of Block made it come to me. I pushed on the pinky ring in the picture and it displayed the steel door.

I punched in the code and went inside Block's personal chambers. I put the combination in all three safes and got the money out. I started putting the money in trash bags to carry to the bedroom. I planned to get an accurate count of the money so when Block and I linked up, I could get info on what to do.

The large stacks were all types of bills from ones, fives, tens, and twenties. The clicking of the bills brought a harsh reality to light. The drugs equaled millions, and the millions created envy. I was under Block's umbrella, so I was a target now. I knew it would be more clowns who tried me. I just had to stay on my toes.

It took me four and a half hours to count all that money. At the end of the clicking, I was surrounded by $10 million liquid cash.

I was speechless as I put the money back into the steel safes. I went back across town to tie up the last of the loose ends. I had set up a meeting between the capos of the organization. I met them down at Cadillac's spot. As I sat in the office, I gave strict orders.

"Now, y'all know we gotta play it safe."

"Play it safe? Is you serious?" one of the soldiers said, venting his frustrations.

"So, what should we do about the work, then? We ain't

get no re-up since Block got knocked," another soldier spoke up.

"I know," I said. "I'm working on that right now. Chances are, they gon' go at our connect. If they do that, don't worry, I got back up plans."

I told them to dump any phones or guns they had. Until further notice, they were to stay out of sight. They weren't happy, but knew the significance of the situation. Everybody knew the drill when the cops started asking questions. You didn't know anything, you didn't see anything, and you weren't saying anything without a lawyer.

I was fielding calls from everybody under the sun. Block's mother called me from a New York number hysterical. I assured her I would be up there as soon as possible. My parents even called me, worried. Block had been a part of our family for a long time. He was my brother. My father knew the game all too well. My mother loved Block as one of her own. I told them all that it would be taken care of.

I hadn't heard from Chante regarding Block. Now, I was a little suspicious of her anyway. I mean, people always seemed to be cool. I thought for sure that she would call. It didn't matter though; I knew what I had to do. I had some of our people clean out her crib. They took the guns that were stashed in the bedroom. What the hell would she tell the cops? She didn't want to be an accessory. The little bit of money she had collected from Block was taken, too. You would never have known Block had ever visited her house. That's the way I wanted it to look anyway.

The week was already exhausting. The good thing was, I only had one more place to go. I had to pick up Block's mother from New York. I made it to the Big Apple in forty-five minutes, looking in my rearview for the cops the entire ride. I parked and took the elevator up to Ms. Sharon's room. She looked worried to death. I noticed she had a pack of cigarettes in her hand. She just came crying into my arms. I stood there and embraced her as she let it all out.

"Why, Swift? Why?" Ms. Sharon repeated over and over again.

"Don't worry about it. He gon' be out in no time. Your boy is a soldier. If anybody can do time, it's Block," I said in her ear.

I led her to my car. When she saw it, she let out a little giggle.

"Where's the Benz?"

"You know I gotta be low key now," I said, starting the Maxima.

I looked over at Ms. Sharon, trying to think what was running through her mind at that moment. Her facial expression wasn't giving much away. She at least seemed relaxed the further we drove. I always had ideas of how I would handle Block being arrested. Talking about it and it actually happening were two totally different things. We sat and discussed it several times. The thing was, I always hoped that it wouldn't come down to this. Now, I felt alone in the world.

Chapter 21
Swift

As soon as I stepped foot inside the court room, it felt weird. The courtroom was loud and almost filled to capacity. Luckily for me, there were a couple of scattered seats remaining along the back wall. I slipped in quietly right as the judge was about to speak.

"Are we ready for the state's opening statement?" he said with a deep baritone.

"Yes, sir. I mean, your honor, we are," District Attorney Jason Caldwell said with a slight smile on his face.

The truth of the matter was that the cops had been trying to pen something on Block for years. He brushed their attempts off every time. Today, however, was something different. I was afraid because it seemed like they had concrete charges. I wasn't saying I didn't believe in Wall Street, but greater things had been pulled off.

I looked over at Block and he wasn't the least bit rattled. The lone diamond in his ear sparkled like Armor All tire spray and the Audemars on his wrist wasn't far behind. The black seersucker suit topped it all off. He looked like new money. That was one of the reasons they hated him. He wasn't over the top. He did his things quietly. He let it bubble until you had to notice. It was like that since I could remember.

We used to run ball back in high school, but Block never wanted to play. They tried to taunt him into playing and it never worked. That was until the day he promptly shut them up with one of the best performances I'd ever saw. He had to drop something like forty points. For the rest of the year, none of the dudes talking trash even looked at Block the wrong way. That was what made Block unique.

I looked at the district attorney and wanted to hurl a chair at him. He looked like the usual dickhead lawyer. It seemed like his suit was too small and his hair had too much gel in it. He kept slicking his hair back, which became annoying after the third time.

It took a minute, but I realized that I knew him from TV. He looked even more like a loser in person. He had a cocky walk to him. Every chance he got, he would cut his eyes at Block. He took a deep breath and approached the juror's box. He was of average height and had a slender build. He adjusted his glasses and turned his attention toward the jury.

"Ladies and gentlemen of the jury, my name is Jason Caldwell, and I wanted to thank you for your joining us today."

I listened to him rant and rave about the monster that Block was. He painted a vivid picture of the destruction he had caused within the so called community. I swore I saw Block laugh a couple times. He even had pictures to bring his point home. When he bought the officer with the broken jaw out, I knew it was over. All I could do was shake my head. The only thing Block did was lean over and whisper something in Wall Street's ear. He quickly scribbled something on the notepad and took a drink of water. The rest of the proceeding seemed to blend together.

All I remember was the judge saying a minimum of thirty six months. The courtroom went ballistic. Block's mother tried to rush past the security guards, but they restrained her. She was kicking and screaming. It broke my heart. I looked over at Trill and Stack and could tell they were affected just as much as I was. The courtroom bench was now cold and uncomfortable. My suit was bringing the claustrophobic side out of me. I adjusted my tie I don't know how many times after he said the verdict.

I saw Block look over at Wall Street and give him a hug. Wall Street whispered something in Block's ear and he nodded. When the officers took Block away, he looked at me dead in the eyes and smiled. It reassured me that everything would be alright.

The courtroom was in a complete uproar. The judge kept banging on the gavel to restore order. Obscenities were being spewed from all directions. The judge barely ducked a shoe that was thrown in his direction. I quickly went over to Block's mother who was sobbing uncontrollably. I sat down and tried to console her as best as I could. I eventually got her to get up and leave with me. I walked out the courtroom just in time to see the press getting ready to enter the building. I could hear the cameras flashing and the questions they were firing away. I went the other way and found the side exit. Block's mother had been through enough for one day. Once she was securely in her car, I walked to the parking garage where my car was.

The walk allowed me to come to terms with the fact that Block was going to jail. I could admit that I was in denial about it. It would be different without him there. I had to think quickly because the cops would be asking questions soon. I walked in the parking garage and took the elevator up to the third floor. I was looking for section G and found it by the back wall.

I sat there for a minute with my eyes closed before I pulled off. I got to the attendant, paid ten dollars, and was back on the street. I saw the media vultures on the steps of the courtroom as I sped by them.

The day had already taken a lot out of me. I needed a drink like yesterday. I drove through the city on autopilot. The heavy tint hid me from onlookers. For the first time in a long time, I welcomed the alone time. It felt like the car was floating me toward my destination. I kept thinking of Natasha's face. I didn't even really know where the hell we were going. All I knew was the feelings I had for her weren't a fluke.

I got to the Old City section of the city and found a rare parking spot. The sidewalk was littered with little tables with white cloths. It was barely enough room for the waiters to get through and the people to sit down. It was humid and I put my suit jacket in the backseat.

Soon as I stepped in the spot, I went straight to the bar. I sidestepped a couple people and finally found a resting place on the stool. The bartender switched herself over to me. I knew I looked like money, but flirting was the furthest thing from my mind at the moment. She bent down to speak and her breasts were inches from my face. I was unfazed. Quite frankly, I was annoyed by it.

"Can I have a rum and Coke? Heavy on the rum."

Sensing I didn't want to play the flirting game, she complied and got to making my drink. While she was making the trek to get my drink, I surveyed the club quickly. The lights flickered on and off as the multiple bodies sashayed to the thunderous records that the DJ spun. It seemed like every girl in the building could see that I had just sent my girl off. I laughed off the notion and spun around in time to grab my drink from the bartender.

The rum burned my throat, and I welcomed it. After a few more, my mind was cloudy and that's the way I wanted it. At that moment, nothing or nobody mattered. I walked out to my car and sat in the driver seat. I punched the dashboard until my hands hurt. The way I was feeling right then, I knew I had to get home before I killed somebody.

That's exactly what I did. I started the engine and drove home. Tomorrow was a new day.

M.Q.W.

Chapter 22
Block

The past couple of days were like nothing Block had ever experienced. He remembered when he was handcuffed and led on to the gray bus on his way to prison. He remembered the uncomfortable green leather seats in the bus. It seemed like the driver went over potholes and speed bumps extra hard on purpose. It was right then when it hit him that he had been caught slipping. He vowed that he would never put himself in that position. The thing was, he couldn't predict the future better than anybody else. He shook his head as he gazed out the window. After a while, all he saw was farm land. His thoughts shifted from his situation to his mother. He knew that this was exactly where she didn't want him to be. She never preached to him about what he did. He already knew what she was thinking.

Her hope was that if he was exposed to different surroundings he could be shaped differently. What she didn't understand was that Block was who he was. The school wasn't going to change that. In a lot of ways, being away at school taught Block a lot about survival. There were a couple instances where kids would try him and fail miserably.

He had always had a knack for selling things. Swift's mother would send Swift a care package full of "outside food." They would break down the stuff and get triple the value of the item. A .25 cent pack of noodles went for a dollar. The people couldn't complain, because either you bought it or you didn't. He made so much money that he had the new Jordan's every October when the season started. Those were the days.

He then thought about Swift and the position he left him in. He knew he could hold it down. He also knew that Pump was still on the streets. That made his blood boil. He put it on his life that when he came home he would make things right.

* * * * *

The sun was hidden by a few clouds in the early morning hours. Two vans slowly crept up the street and turned on to the expensive property. The van door slid open and black suit clad agents hopped out with guns drawn. The two front seat passengers went to get the battering ram from the back of the van. The remaining agents followed behind the lead agent walking slowly up the steps.

"On my count...One...two...three." Putting their weight behind it, the front door flew off the hinges and slid into the bottom steps. The morning sun shone brightly inside the foyer now. Machine guns equipped with infrared lasers crisscrossed each other as the agents swarmed the house, covering every inch of the small mansion. They followed closely behind one another until they reached the top of the stairs. When they went upstairs, they slowed down, seeing that the couple was still asleep. The first agent found it odd that they slept through all the noise.

The minute the agents relaxed, Caliente grabbed the Glock .40 from his nightstand drawer and his wife, Sierra, grabbed the shotgun from under the bed. Before the agents could protect themselves, shots exploded. Caliente and Sierra had no intentions of going to jail. Sierra's shotgun blast put two agents through the wooden banister and down the stairs.

Caliente wasn't too far behind, putting a few agents down himself. While the agents were stunned, they made their move toward the bathroom, still shooting. As Sierra ran across the carpet, a shot hit her shoulder. Bullets nearly took Caliente and Sierra's heads off as they approached the bathroom.

Caliente and Sierra went into the elevator that doubled as a linen closet. The elevator led to the basement level garage. They made sure to grab extra bullets. They both hopped into a black Hummer and reloaded before they sped off.

When they crashed through the garage door, more agents awaited them. As soon as they saw black uniforms, they started squeezing again. Sierra was one-handing the shotgun with her right hand and steering with the left. It was like the gunshot wound wasn't affecting her at all. She was knocking agents down like bowling pins. That was until one of the snipers on the roof top put a bullet through her forehead. It caused the Hummer to swerve into the side of the house.

Caliente kissed his gold cross, and then his wife's deceased hand. He said a silent prayer before grabbing the street sweeper off the backseat. He jammed in the clip and peeked out the window. The agents were closing in. Caliente got out and hid behind the driver side door. The barrel of his gun looked like fireworks as it spit bullets. He managed to wound more agents in the process.

But, he didn't even stand a chance with the firepower they were packing. The infrared lights illuminated Caliente's white bathrobe, turning it burgundy red. The agents had no sympathy as they gunned him down with everything they had.

He was on one knee, laughing hysterically as the bullets tore through his flesh easily. With his last bit of strength, he tried one more time to aim his gun, his hand shaking. The agent he was aiming at pulled a handgun and put him out his misery. The final bullet left a stump where his head used to be. Caliente fell forward, still holding the gun.

When the shots concluded, Caliente and his wife had killed over a dozen agents. The agents proceeded to scour the grounds, coming up empty on anything useful. They had been on Caliente a little over a week. What they couldn't figure out was how they had witnessed him bring in drugs and money, yet there was no trace of either one.

The lead agent pulled out his cell and waited for his call to be answered.

"Servonte speaking."

"Hello, Detective, I need you and Stokes down here right away. You're going to love this."

"We're on our way."

* * * * *

Bird sat with Bear, Thoro, and Speed inside Fat Tuesday's on South Street. They all toasted to their new start. They were celebrating Block's arrest.

"Block is lucky I didn't kill his nut ass personally. He got out the easy way," Bird said before sipping on his drink. The rest of the time, they sat around laughing and joking for hours on end. When the men had enough to drink, they left the building.

The truck wasn't far from where they were. When they got close to it, a tall figure approached the vehicle, gripping a gun. Bear immediately pushed Bird down to the ground and pulled his gun. Thoro and Speed never got a chance to follow suit. Mav killed both of them with the P94 he was carrying. He was intent on spraying everything out there.

Bear emptied his clip while peeking around the truck. Mav returned bullets, leaving dents in the passenger side of the truck. Bear took a moment to reload, trying to keep his eye on where Mav was.

When he went to look up again, a barrel was pressed behind his ear. He froze, waiting for something to happen. Mav's face creased into a devilish smile. Soon as he heard police sirens, he panicked. He fired a wild shot, cracking the windshield of the police car. The first cop out of the car returned fire immediately.

Seeing as though now he had started a gun fight, he had to escape. He ran around the back of the car to give himself a shield. He peeked around the truck and put a few more bullets into the door of the cop car. When he went to shoot again, the gun clicked empty. He looked down at it in disbelief. He looked around frantically and noticed a gate. If he could time it right, he could escape. He looked again and noticed that innocent bystanders who heard the shots were now crowding the small space where they were. Seeing his opportunity arise, Mav hopped over the gate like a pole vaulter.

It wasn't the first time he got chased by the cops. It probably wouldn't be the last. He looked down the alleyway and saw the cop car speeding by. He crossed the street and was running as fast as he could. He could see one of the brave cops was on his heels. No matter how many times he made a short cut or zig zagged, the cop was on top of him. He turned the corner just in time to see someone about to come out of their house. He pushed them back in and slammed the door shut. The elderly white lady didn't want to anger the angry black man with the huge gun, so she sat right on her couch. Mav peeked out the window and saw the cop looking around and even under the cars. After ten minutes of searching, he spoke into his shoulder walkie talkie. He could hear the crackle of the other voice on the other end. When the cop car came and picked up the officer, Mav was relieved.

He slid down the wall temporarily forgetting where he

was.

"I'm so sorry, ma'am" Mav said waving the gun absently.

Mav pulled out $200 and handed it to the now smiling old lady. He peeked out the door and was satisfied that the coast was clear. He tucked the gun in his waist and walked back through South Philly 'til he came across the subway. He tried to walk normal as possible. He swore that they were waiting right on the train for him. He paid the attendant and went through the turnstile. The subway car came roaring past on the other side before the West Bound train stopped in front of Mav. Mav blended in with the crowd of people exiting the train. He sat down in the first available orange seat. He knew he had escaped the law yet again.

* * * * *

Chante was really furious at her present situation. Both of her breadwinners were in limbo. She was Caramel to Bird and Chante to Block. She had tight roped the act for long enough. She knew Block would eventually catch on. She cursed herself for getting caught up. She was salty to find her house had been raided. She knew Block was cautious, but didn't know how severe. As she looked through her closet, she thought, *God, they didn't take my chinchilla coat with the hood.* She grabbed her Coach bag and was out the door.

She hopped in her silver Mercedes coupe and decided to go on a shopping spree. She figured at least she would hit him in the pockets if nothing else. She knew that money was really Block's world. She loved him, but she was far from stupid. The ride to the bank wasn't long at all. She found a close parking spot and fed the meter before she walked across the street.

She walked in the bank like she owned it. Her nose was in the air and she wanted everybody to know that she was privileged. Her attitude was on full display.

"Hello, how may I help you?"

"You can help me by directing me to the safe deposit boxes."

"What the name is the box under, ma'am?"

"Johnson."

"And the first name?"

"Rickey."

Although she was scanning the list for less than thirty seconds, Chante thought it was an eternity.

"I'm sorry, ma'am, we don't have anything under that name."

She let out a sarcastic laugh.

"Let me look again."

"Yeah, you do that."

"I'm sorry, bu—"

"I want the manager, now," Chante shouted, causing heads to turn.

"No problem. I will get him right away."

The bank teller walked off to the corner office and came out with a fat, balding black man.

"Is there a problem?"

"I'll tell you the problem. I have over ten thousand dollars in this bank and I want it now."

"Ok. Ok. Let me personally check the list."

The manager looked over the list with a fine toothed comb and came up with the same results.

"I'm sorry, ma— " He cut himself off. "What was the name again?"

"Rickey Johnson," Chante said, even more annoyed.

"I regret to inform you Mr. Johnson took that money out a few days ago."

"How the hell is that possible when his black ass is in jail? You tell me that, you fat bastard."

Two hulk like security guards came out and dragged Chante outside. She dusted herself off, hoping the instant headache she just developed would go away.

She noticed she had a ticket. She snatched the pink slip and stuffed it into her Coach bag. She hopped into the car and drove back home, defeated. Soon as she got into the house, she looked in the cupboard and got her favorite nose candy. She sat in front of the line of cocaine, staring into space. When she did a couple lines, she had quickly forgotten her misfortunes.

Instead, she was thinking of a way to bribe Block. Since plan A didn't pan out, she had to go for plan B. She just knew she had some key information on him. She just didn't know how much money she wanted for it. The drugs had her really tripping. It was a habit she picked up from Bird. She grabbed the phone to dial the precinct.

When she went down for another sniff, a shotgun pressed against her scalp. Stack wasted no time redecorating her furniture in bright red.

CHAPTER 23
SWIFT

I was up unusually early and knew it was due to how things had been going lately. I got ready for my day like I normally did. After I got dressed, I put the tea kettle on the stove on high. I grabbed the instant coffee and poured two spoonfuls in my coffee cup. I added the cream and sugar, and waited for the whistle to sound. I cut on the plasma TV in the kitchen and the news was on. It seemed like Caliente's death had turned into a mini series. Every news outlet we had did a story on it. I changed the channel to Comcast Sportsnet. I walked past the couch and nudged Mav to wake him up. He mumbled something inaudible and I continued on toward the kitchen.

When my cousin showed up at the door sweating like a fugitive with a gun on his waist, I knew it was a problem. I had to get him as far away as possible. He already had two strikes and they were itching to give him another one. He didn't even make it to the guest room. He collapsed right on the couch.

I got my caffeine fix for the day and after I checked the receipts and totals for the week, I went upstairs to get the money ready.

I heard Mav's terrible singing in the shower. I looked at

my Audemars and noticed Trill would be here any minute. The minute I got to the top of the steps I heard him walk in.

"I got ya message. You ready?

"Yeah. I'm just waiting for Mav to get dressed."

"Aight, I'ma start the car."

I made sure all the lights were off before I walked to the front door. Mav was coming down the steps at the same time with the suitcases. When he went through, I closed and locked the door.

I got outside and Trill was smoking a cigarette. When he saw me, he threw the cigarette in the street and opened the back door. I hopped in while Mav put the suitcases in the trunk. Trill pulled off and we were on our way to State Road. We pulled up to the prison parking lot, and Trill parked in the first spot that opened up.

I went through the metal detector and signed the necessary papers so I could finally speak to Block. Just as I was getting to the visiting area, Block strolled in at the same time escorted by a CO. We sat down, picked up the phones, and started talking.

"What's good, baby boy?" Block said.

"Holding it down. You know I got Wall Street working on your case night and day."

"I know. I appreciate that a whole lot," Block said. "There ain't nobody else I trust at all like that anyway. You know how I am."

"You know I know."

"As you know, I'm down for a minute. Ain't nothing to a boss though. We gon' need a new coach since homie got fired," Block said, referring to Caliente's demise.

"I think we got somebody lined up for the position," I said, looking Block directly in his eyes.

"Make that happen."

"Done." We talked for ten minutes before the guard

butted in.

"Obviously, my time's up," Block said. "You know how these guards is. It's your turn to step up. Show 'em what time it is."

"I got you," I said, pressing my fist up to the glass separating us. Block pressed his fist up in return. I watched my partner walk back through the door and knew that the adjustment period had just begun. I made the walk back through the facility and into the parking lot. Trill fired up the Maybach when he saw me coming.

I got in and was a little nervous riding around the city with that much money in the trunk. I kept checking the refrigerator in the Maybach to make sure my gun was still there.

"I can't stand them punk ass security guards," Trill said, pulling out the parking lot.

"You know they only do that 'cause it makes 'em feel like a tough guy, right."

"I got they tough guy right here," Trill said, patting the glove compartment.

After about a half hour, we pulled into a deserted parking lot. There was grass growing out of the concrete and the gates surrounding it were bent out of place with barbwire on top of them. There were bright light poles in the four corners of the lot, spotlighting the private jet that was sitting there.

Trill pulled alongside it and killed the engine. He popped the trunk, and then he and Mav helped me with the suitcases. The stewardess extended the stairs and walked us in. We put them on the plane and walked back to the car. Before I stepped off, Trill gave me the dap and hug combo. I trusted Trill with my life, and I couldn't say that about many people. Trill was an unorthodox dude. He would bust you upside your head quick, but would help an old lady with her groceries. That's what made him Trill though.

Me and Mav were walking to the plane when I heard the

engine start up. That's when Trill spoke.

"Ay, Swift, you got that lighter?"

I dug in my pocket and underhand threw it to him.

"Good lookin', baby. Be safe, my dude. One." Trill pulled out, leaving long tire marks across the gray asphalt.

The stewardess came out to see if we needed any further assistance. We walked up the steps and the stewardess ushered us to our seats. She went back and pressed the button, sending the stairs upward. The plane sat eight people comfortably. The interior was champagne colored and the carpeting matched. There was a flat screen TV behind every seat with earphone inputs. There was actually foot space. Being 6'2, I really appreciated it.

I didn't notice home girl before, but she was busting out of her uniform. Her hair was cut short and curled up. Her lips had a permanent pout covered in red lipstick. Her shirt was cut low and revealed just enough to get you interested. Her deep dimples and banana skin complexion were turning me on. As she walked to the back, she flashed a dentist approved smile.

After a few moments, she came back with a bucket of ice holding a bottle of Ace of Spades. She popped the cork with minimum splashing. She handed me the bottle and sashayed to the back again. I offered Mav some and he declined. I drank half the bottle and decided to take a short nap. We had a long flight ahead of us.

* * * * *

Nice Cote D'Azur Airport in Saint Tropez was packed with people. We walked through the airport, taking in the sights and sounds of the culture. Almost everybody that I saw had on beach clothes. Women had bikini tops, and the guys had on cargo shorts and shades. We dragged the suitcases, making use of the wheels, and went straight to the double doors. The sun was bright and there was no sign of a breeze in the immediate future.

The dark gray Sequoia was parked across the street and a man was holding a sign with my name. We strolled over, and the guy took the suitcases and put them in the trunk. Me and Mav hopped in the backseat. The man got in the driver's seat and we pulled off. The architecture of the buildings in Saint Tropez was beautiful and perfectly sculptured. Just to see another culture left me speechless. Kids ran up and down the sidewalks playing with soccer balls. They had hustlers on the street hawking everything from fruit to incense sticks.

We got to our destination in less than twenty minutes. The beige and brown colored villa sat on its own and was situated on top of a hill with a spectacular view of the water. The water seemed to sparkle when the sunlight hit it. With the city as a backdrop, it looked like it was supposed to be on a postcard. The driver got out and opened the back door for us.

We got the suitcases out the car and put them in the house. I gave Mav two sets of keys. One for the house and one for the car parked in the driveway. I nearly forgot to give him the card to withdraw money. I could see in Mav's face that he didn't want to really be down there. He knew that his options were limited. He had been to jail already and didn't plan on going back again. He wasn't really an emotional dude, but he gave me a long hug just before I left.

"Cousin," I said, "don't let nothing happen to this money. Block won't hesitate to have you killed."

"I would never put you in that position. You done more for me than I could ever ask for."

"It's nothing. You just make sure to lay low and stay off the radar. Dig me?"

"I got you," Mav said as I gave him dap one more time.

I walked back outside and got into the backseat of the

truck. Knowing that my cousin was safe put me at ease, which was good considering life was about to do a one-eighty on me. With Block in jail, things were going to be different. I was used to being able to speed dial his number and get at him. I was used to seeing him running things, but now it was time for me to man-up and take the reins. The streets were definitely watching, and I wasn't going to let them or Block down. I knew this was my time to shine or get shined on, and I planned to be the brightest thing out there - for Block and for me.

Meet The Author

Born November 21, 1984 in Philadelphia, PA, Markeise Q. Washington has been writing since he was ten years old. In late 2006 his literary journey began when he started penning his debut novel "Entrepreneur". With his mind set on ownership, 5ive Star Publications was born in May 2007. His goal was to cover all genres of fiction as well as children's literature.

Destined and encouraged to do great things Markeise is constantly reminded of the early and unfortunate passing of his biological mother whom is indeed the catalyst to his success. Proactive, determined, thought provoking and intelligent, Markeise Q. Washington will always and forever remind us that "Dreams are today's answers to tomorrow's questions".

BRUTHAS

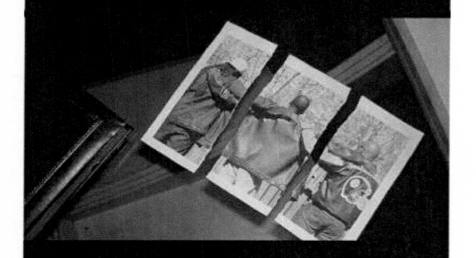

A NOVEL BY J.L. WHITEHEAD

 WWW.5IVESTARPUBLICATIONS.COM

Lady Vicious

A NOVEL BY
VICTORIA VANEE' ANDERSON

 WWW.5IVESTARPUBLICATIONS.COM

Through Her Eyes

A Novel by
Krystol

 WWW.5IVESTARPUBLICATIONS.COM

South side Hustler

Robert "Rala" Jackson Kenneth "K-Love" Davis Marvin "Biz" Harrigan

Richard "Rick" Burton Craig "Money" Stanford Jermaine "Kells" Kelson

*The pictures on the cover are not depicted in the book.
The book cover is dedicated to their memory and the families of many others.
The families of the loved ones approved the usage of their imagery.

A NOVEL BY RICH MCLAUGHLIN

www.5ivestarpublications.com

Entrepreneur II:
THE TRANSITION

A NOVEL BY M.Q.W.

 WWW.5IVESTARPUBLICATIONS.COM

5IVE STAR PUBLICATIONS
P.O. BOX 9176
WILMINGTON, DE 19809

DATE:

PURCHASER:

MAILING ADDRESS:

CITY:

STATE: **ZIP CODE:**

Qty	Title Of Book	Price Each	Total
	Entrepreneur	13.00	
	Entrepreneur II: The Transition	13.00	
	Lady Vicious*	15.00	
	Bruthas*	15.00	
	Through Her Eyes*	13.00	
	Southside Hustler	15.00	
	Total Books Ordered	Subtotal	
	(Priority Mail $5.25 each) (If ordering more than one add $ 2.00 each)	Shipping	
	Institutional Check and Money Orders	Total	
	(No Personal Checks)		

* Coming Soon

ATTENTION BOOKSTORES

TO PURCHASE BOOKS FROM 5IVE STAR PUBLICATIONS

Through The Publishing Company

Call For Additional Information And Wholesale Pricing

Contact: Keith Washington, Washington Marketing Group 215-833-8502

Or

Visit:
www.5ivestarpublications.com

Breinigsville, PA USA
13 April 2011
259661BV00001B/9/P